EXPECTING GOODNESS

EXPECTING GOODNESS

& other stories

THE ESSENTIAL FICTION OF SPARTANBURG

edited by C. MICHAEL CURTIS

HUB CITY PRESS
SPARTANBURG, SC

First printing, December 2009

Editorial Assistant: Patrick Whitfill
Proofreaders: Carol Bradof, Candace
Lamb, Jameelah Lang, Jan Scalisi,
Betsy Teter, and George Williams
Book design: Emily Smith
Cover photograph © Joel Sartore for
National Geographic

Library of Congress
Cataloging-in-Publication Data

Expecting Goodness & Other Stories :
the Essential Fiction of Spartanburg /
edited by C. Michael Curtis.
p. cm.
ISBN 978-1-891885-70-9
(pbk. : alk. paper)
1.   Short stories, American—South
     Carolina—Spartanburg.
2.   Spartanburg (S.C.)—Fiction.
I.   Curtis, C. Michael.
II. Hub City Writers Project.
III. Title: Expecting goodness and
     other stories.
PS559.S73E97 2009
813'.0108975729—dc22
2009027720

Hub City Press
149 S. Daniel Morgan Avenue
Suite 2
Spartanburg, SC 29306
864.577.9349 · 864.577.0188
www.hubcity.org

TABLE OF CONTENTS

INTRODUCTION

➢ C. MICHAEL CURTIS

Seamus Heaney once wrote of the poetic imagination he sought to encourage that it "sings very close to the music of what happened." To suggest that the fiction of Spartanburg verges on "the music of what happened" is not far-fetched, though current thinking about form in the short story challenges hard ideas about both musicality and event.

In most of the stories gathered here "something happens," a characteristic that puts them at some remove from the static, minutely observed, sometimes fantastical stories beloved by many writers and, self-evidently, by their editors. In certain respects, the "dynamic" fiction in these stories takes us back to traditional forms and purposes. It also satisfies, however, what seems to me a natural characteristic of storytelling: to surround an event with its apparent causes and consequences, and to focus attention on the principal actors in the unfolding drama.

Many of the writers earn their keep in one or another of Spartanburg's educational edifices—Deno Trakas, John Lane, Elizabeth Cox, and Jeremy Jones at Wofford College; Sam Howie, Kathryn A. Brackett, and Susan Tekulve at Converse College; and Tom McConnell and Marilyn Knight at USC Upstate. Others, like Michel Stone and Lou Dischler, circulate freely in Spartanburg's literary mainstream and write both diligently and well. A few younger writers, like Thomas Pierce, Molly Knight, and Chris Bundy, are in school or working elsewhere. One Spartanburg veteran, Rosa Shand, who taught at both Wofford and Converse, now lives and works in Davidson, North Carolina. The others, Carol Isler, Wendy King, Kam Neely, Norman Powers, and Betty Burgin Snow, are writers whose work is not widely known but ought to be.

But why this anthology? And why should I, a relative newcomer to Spartanburg, be its hunter and gatherer? To answer the last question first, I'm a habitual anthologist (this is my seventh), perhaps because I've been a magazine fiction editor for more than forty-five years and so have an attachment to the form. Since coming to Spartanburg more than three years ago to teach at Wofford, I've enjoyed the company of most of the writers collected here, and I leaped at the chance to pull together a sampling of their best work. In my imagination, this book will never be out of print. It will be everyone's favorite Christmas present, a required text for book discussion groups in every church in the Upstate, mandatory reading in high school English classes, and the declared favorite reading of NASCAR drivers, Beacon habitués, high school sports enthusiasts, and every other major population group identified by political pollsters. Who could do without it?

This collection will not launch a revival of interest in fiction here in Spartanburg; that revival is already well under way. What it *will* do is underline the depth and quality of the writing in our midst. These stories do, in important ways, celebrate the "music of what happened."

C. Michael Curtis is Fiction Editor of The Atlantic, *where he has worked for forty-six years. He also shares with his wife, Elizabeth Cox, the John C. Cobb Chair in the Humanities at Wofford College. He is the editor of six other story anthologies, including* God Stories *and* Faith Stories *(Houghton Mifflin) and has published poetry, reviews, and essays in* The Atlantic, The New Republic, The National Review, *and many other publications.* ✳

EXPECTING GOODNESS

LOLA'S PRAYER

➤ LOU DISCHLER

As Lola was driving back from the beach she noticed a farmer's truck parked in the weeds alongside the road, a sign with drippy red lettering leaning against the fender. It said:

BREED CHINCHILLAS!
MAKE YOUR OWN FUR COAT!
ONLY $15.00!

Breeding normally required two animals, of course, but the female she bought was pregnant, so she was already saving fifteen dollars. The farmer boxed it up and put it on her backseat. How it got out she didn't know, but she hadn't driven very far before she noticed it between her feet, peering up at her with its beady black eyes. She screamed, it screamed, and the car veered off the road and ran into a ditch. Fortunately, the ditch was shallow, and with some spinning of tires she managed to free herself. When she got home, one side of her car was splattered with mud, and the frightened chinchilla was nowhere to be found. She searched everywhere, under the seats, in the glove box. No chinchilla. The next day she told this story as she was typing up a requisition, and Bethany Ann, who was filing her fingernails at the next desk, said her boyfriend Jimmy had a snake get loose in his truck. And not just some old garden snake. A yellow ring neck.

"Is that poisonous?"

"Poisonous! It's only the most poisonous snake in the world. Worse

1

than a cobra. Jimmy had to wear his steel-toe boots every day, 'cause if it bit him they'd have to saw off his leg."

"Why saw it off?" said Billy Ray, who did all the filing and had a crush on Bethany Ann. "They could just put a tourniquet around his neck."

Bethany Ann narrowed her eyes. "You should've been a doctor, Billy Ray, smart boy like you."

Billy Ray grinned and winked.

"Did he ever find it?" Lola asked.

"Yeah, eventually. Coiled up in the glove box. Imagine finding a yellow ring neck coiled up in your glove compartment. I'd've died."

Lola stopped typing and looked over at her. "I already checked the glove box. Wasn't in there."

"You're lucky you didn't get bit."

"For God's sake, Bethany Ann. It's just a chinchilla."

"Let me clue you in, sugar. Chinchillas ain't nothing but rats, and rats are even worse than snakes. They'll squeeze in anywhere and eat anything. You remember how a wharf rat ate that baby's lips in New Jersey? Ate 'em plum off."

"I never heard that—"

"And wasn't much left of his nose and ears. Just those little nubs."

"Good grief, Bethany Ann."

"Hey, I'm just saying. Read the *Enquirer* if you wanna get educated."

Lola found this conversation troubling, and for the rest of the day she was plagued with images of a rat-like chinchilla yanking foam from her seats, or worse, chomping on bundles of wires with its rat teeth, destroying vital automotive organs. That evening she used the mirror of her compact to inspect the undercarriage. What she saw there was as mysterious to her as the wrong side of the moon, but she found no trace of chinchilla except for a few hairs lodged in the tailpipe. She plucked them and rolled them in her fingers. Dark brown and gray—could these be chinchilla hairs? Could an animal have squeezed in there? Could it even *live* in there? She knelt and squinted into the black depths of the pipe. The sudden thought of a snarling beast jumping out and biting her nose sent her sprawling on the asphalt where she tore the seat of her almost-new Catalina slacks and skinned her elbows.

Fuming now, she stomped inside her house, dabbed her wounds with a paper towel dipped in mustard, then placed a call to her sister in Alabama. Could a chinchilla live in your tailpipe, she wanted to know. Her sister referred the question to her husband, who was a hunter and therefore knew where animals could or couldn't live. Lola heard the muffled exchange, then her sister came back on and repeated the gist of what her husband had said, that no fucking way could anything live in your exhaust system, and furthermore, was she an idiot? Lola said thank you and next time she'd ask somebody else.

On Tuesday she found more hair in the tailpipe, and her car began to moan like the garbage truck that hauled away her trash. The chinchilla was destroying her car!

She drove to the Sell Quick on Fraser Street and bought a trap designed for catching mice inside walls. It had a pull-string so you could pull it out, and it was slim so it would slip into a narrow hole. Still, it didn't quite fit the exhaust pipe, but she was able to pound it in with a brick. Later, she drove to an outlet mall on the interstate to buy a new pair of slacks. In the parking lot she checked again—no chinchilla, but the shiny white plastic of the trap had turned a velvety black, and the pull-string was gone. She didn't want to jump to conclusions, but suspected the chinchilla had eaten it.

At the food court she bought a lunch of barbecued chicken fingers and Mountain Dew and sat at one of the tables. It was nearly noon, noisy and crowded, and she'd barely taken her knife and fork from its plastic wrapper when a man with a tray asked if she minded. She saw there weren't any open tables so she nodded—one of those grudging half-nods that told anyone with a lick of sense they could sit there, but no way were they sitting *together*.

"You work at the paper mill in Georgetown, don't you?" he said after a while. "In the office?"

"What?" Lola said, glancing up. "Were you speaking to me?"

"I'm sorry. My name's Henry." He extended his hand across the table. "Henry Dutton."

"I don't believe I know you," she said coldly, and turned back to her food.

He made no further effort at conversation, and Lola refused to look in his direction until he left. Mr. Dutton might have been nice enough, but one never knew. He might be the sort to cut her up and pickle her ovaries in a jar—what a drycleaner had done in New Orleans, according to Bethany Ann. Lola became so distracted by this encounter that she forgot about the chinchilla.

Not until two days later, coming out of the Wal-Mart Supercenter did she remember to check. To her dismay the trap was gone, and now there was even more hair. When she turned onto her street in Georgetown, her car's moaning turned brassy, like a pair of trombones. She twisted the radio all the way up, jerked the wheel, and made a U-turn. She drove to the edge of town, where she finally rolled into tall yellow grass in front of a white clapboard house with a wooden cross planted in the yard. When she cut the engine, silence roared in her ears.

"I ain't one for fixing cars," said Madame Mozzie. She was an elderly and emaciated black woman who squinted so much she appeared to be blind. "I fix de men, not de cars. De men, you know what I say?"

"I know," Lola said. "I just want to get the chinchilla out."

"Why don't you go to de Exxon for dat? Dey get it out."

"I have my reasons," Lola said. Which were mostly that she didn't want to see the man she'd dated three years before. Jed Harmsworth was a ruddy-faced mechanic who liked to work with his hands, while Lola was a pale, thirty-year-old virgin with double D-cups, an untenable combination.

Madame Mozzie gave Lola a bottle of juice for ridding one's domicile of unwanted lovers, saying it would work on chinchillas so long as you whacked them with a gris-gris stick when they came out. Whack them, otherwise your domicile could become re-infested. The juice was free, but the stick was twenty dollars. It looked just like a length of lumber to Lola, but she wasn't a carpenter or a practitioner of voodoo.

"And you must say a prayer to de Virgin Mary."

"I'm not bothering the Virgin Mary with a chinchilla."

"You must. She take de man wid her. Dey all pray for dat."

"What man? We're talking about animals, right?"

Mozzie wiggled her fingers dismissively. "Vermin, all one'n de same."

She nodded toward a concrete sculpture of the Madonna in the corner, right next to the door. "You can say de prayer before you leave."

But Lola didn't pray to the concrete Madonna, and, frankly, she was put off by Mozzie's dictatorial manner. Lola had noticed how people did things just because they were told to do them. Like changing their oil every three months or three thousand miles. Lola hadn't changed her oil in three years, ever since she broke up with Jed. Fifty thousand miles without an oil change and her Toyota still hummed along—if you overlooked the trumpeting from the pipes and the occasional chewing sounds, but that couldn't be blamed on oil. The juice would work without bothering the Virgin Mary, and the chinchilla would find some other place to live. She couldn't explain how she knew these things. She just knew.

"You'll find a better home," she said as she pulled up in front of her house. "How about a Mercedes. Would you like that?"

This question was answered only by the neighbor's dog, an ancient corgi that ran figure eights behind its Hurricane fence, barking each time it turned around, which it did whenever Lola came home. Now Lola edged her Toyota toward the curb, slowly running it back and forth as she studied the curb in her side view. She didn't want to get too close and risk damaging her tires—which were bald and bulging ominously—and she didn't want her car poking out in the street where some uninsured maniac might slam into it. She also wanted to be equidistant from each end of the property line, to prevent others from parking there. What if someone parked there to live? Whole families from Charleston were living in cars nowadays because of the economic downturn. And one Saturday just a month ago, two full-sized cars had squeezed into her little space. She'd left notes under their windshield wipers, then watched until the drivers returned. Both left without noticing the folded paper. But they would, she'd thought. They would read her notes and they would never park there again. She'd written:

> I'm sure you did not mean to be rude, but this is my private property. If you would be ever so kind to be more considerate in the future, please park in Charleston or

wherever you come from. Your cooperation in this matter is appreciated.

She never saw them again, and she'd felt a sense of achievement, having addressed this problem herself. Now in her bedroom, she slipped on old blue jeans, a stained sweat shirt, and went back out to her car carrying the stick and bottle of potion. She opened the bottle and sniffed the dark red oil, which reminded her of paprika and rotten bananas. She sprinkled a little experimentally, watching it splat darkly on the asphalt. She used up half the bottle making a protective circle around the Toyota, then poured a goodly amount in the tailpipe. Some of it flowed inside, toward the chinchilla, but most of it dribbled on the ground. This worried her. She wiped around the rim with her finger, noticing how oily black it was, and was suddenly amazed that she'd stuck her finger in that hole without thinking. No telling what diseases were brewing in there! Rodents weren't careful where they went to the bathroom, and now she suspected the black on her finger was excrement. Dizzy with revulsion, she held her finger out in front of her and ran to the house, where she scrubbed her fingers with detergent, then with bleach. Later, lying in bed in her underwear, she listened to the sonorous sound of the dishwasher as it worked on a load, imagining Mozzie's potion making the same sound as it flushed vermin from her car.

But the juice didn't work. The next afternoon Lola found even more hair in the tailpipe, and the engine was louder and throatier than ever. This seemed more than one chinchilla could accomplish, and a new worry took hold: had the chinchilla given birth? Was it using the carburetor as a nursery?

She shivered at the thought. An hour later she impulsively picked up her phone and began dialing the Exxon station, then slammed it down. No way would she put up with those big hands of Jed's, always touching her, even on the breasts. "I'm sorry," he would say with his goofy smile, pretending it was an accident. "I'm just a bit clumsy." But this was a lie, for she'd seen how he was with the intricate parts of his fishing reel. Those big hands weren't clumsy at all. She covered her chest with her arms, thinking of his touch, and her shoulders jerked with a sudden revulsion. She wouldn't call him; she'd solve this problem on her own.

She decided the juice had failed because the chinchillas had gotten into the engine, which she imagined as sort of a hotel in miniature, with a warren of steamy hallways and tiny rooms, each home to a wiggling chinchilla baby. After some difficulty finding the latch, she sprung the hood and stared at the bizarre arrangement of boxes and pipes that was entirely meaningless to her. She counted nine capped openings that led into the depths of the engine. Opening one after another, she divided the remaining juice between them, then recapped the holes and closed the hood. After wiping her hands on a rag, she sat behind the wheel with Mozzie's stick. She was pleased with herself, for she'd worked on the engine just as a mechanic would have. Just as Jed would have . . . but no, she wouldn't think of him.

The evening was sultry but mosquito free, so she rolled down the windows and passed the time with a tabloid. Every so often she glanced around, but nothing was moving. Darkness fell and cicadas began their buzzing. A truck rattled by with only its parking lights on. She watched it suspiciously until it disappeared, then took a lighter from her pocket and circled her vehicle. By the flickering light she saw dim shapes darting to and fro, but after a few swings with the stick, she decided this was her imagination. She got down on her knees and held the lighter underneath, waving the stick in a threatening manner. She expected chinchillas to scurry out like roaches, but again she was disappointed. She stood and noticed a tomcat strolling up the sidewalk toward her, its green eyes glowing like jewels. She popped the stick twice on the concrete; the cat hissed and ran away with a long, loping stride. Minutes passed, still no chinchillas. Finally she gave up and went inside.

The next morning the noises had grown. She turned off the radio for a moment and listened to the engine for the first time in days. Such a racket of clicking and moaning! In desperation she stopped at the Sell Quick and bought an ivory statute of the Virgin Mary for seven ninety-five. She placed it on the slanted vinyl of the dash. Its smooth eyes stared at her impassively, two fingers of its right hand offering an eternal benediction. Like most Catholics, Lola believed that animals didn't go to heaven, so she prayed to this plastic Madonna to make an exception: *Just this once, Mother of God, take the chinchillas.*

But either the Madonna wasn't listening or Lola lacked sufficient grace, for when she started the engine, its clunks and groans were just as bad. Even though the early morning was cool, the air in her car was stifling, and she now feared the engine might burst into flames. Which was why she didn't turn onto the access road to the paper mill as she usually did on a weekday. Instead she continued up the highway until she saw the glowing sign for the Exxon station. Jed was already at work, kneeling on the wide apron of pavement, head down, intent on a gray lump of machinery. When she slowed, her car let out a double blast of trumpets. Jed looked up; his eyes locked onto hers. He raised one of his big hands, black with oil and grease, and Lola suddenly realized what a terrible mistake she was making. She punched the accelerator; the Toyota's engine shuddered with an explosion. A great pall of smoke twisted in her rearview, and a moment later everything behind her was swallowed up.

Now miles down the road, Lola's Toyota was still moaning, but perhaps not as badly as before. The scent of rotten bananas filled the air, and she wondered: had the chinchillas been vaporized? Or had they been taken? She touched the Madonna, turned the radio up, and soon was singing along. ✳

SWEETNESS

> ROSA SHAND

— — — — — — — — — —

I'm going back to the fifties to tell this part of my life. It's a part which almost no one has admitted to knowing.

I was eleven years old. My father was holding the door and telling me, "Hurry up, Sweetness." My name was Mary Wright, not *Sweetness*, but my father called me whatever he felt like. He walked partway to school with me. My mother stayed in bed because her play rehearsals—hers and Brandy's—kept her up at night (Brandy was my mother's orange-headed friend).

When we came to Marna's house, my father turned off to his office on Broad and I went on with Marna, who was my one friend. We ducked the Pritchards' vines but Marna caught her pigtail in a branch. I waited while she untangled herself and we walked on, me looking down, missing the cracks on the sidewalk.

Out of the blue she said, "Did you know your mother and Brandy were lovers?"

She said it as if she were telling me something sick and she didn't have the good sense to drop the subject. She said, "Well, did you know?"

I said, "A person says *lovers* when it's a man and a woman. Women are friends. *Friends* means loving each other."

"I knoooow." She dragged out the *o*, as if she knew and I didn't.

"So why say what you said?"

"I heard it."

"You heard what from who?"

"My mother and Mrs. Guerry. They said it like it was something everybody knew."

"Of course everybody knows. Brandy is my mother's friend *and* she's my father's friend and *mine* if you haven't noticed. You too—you think she's funny."

"So?"

I sped up my walking. She sped up. I despised her. I warned her: "If you say what you said to anybody else alive I will not be your friend. Never. I swear on the Bible."

She pretended she was puzzled. She said, "You don't have to be mad."

For maybe a week I didn't walk with her or talk to her. I took my father a different way, not by Marna's house. I told him I had outgrown Marna and that was the way life was.

What I suspected: being with just my father was better and safer. Even when my mother was with my father and me, I was uneasy. My mother would be looking at her food or out the window and my father would be trying to catch her attention, staring at her big black droopy eyes as if he couldn't help himself (Marna told me once my mother's eyes were *sexy*). My father's staring at her always left me begging my mother under my breath: Make my father happy. Please. Just look at him every now and then. Please. Wherever we were, I'd be watching her, hoping she would glance up at my father.

Usually, when my father came home from work, he and my mother and Brandy and every now and then somebody else would have their cocktails out in the back, out in the garden my father'd made and stubbornly plotted and weeded—he persisted in trying to interest my mother in his strange streaked daffodils and velvet-red petunias. Mostly he and Brandy carried on the conversations because Brandy talked the way men talked, about how the country needed a president, not a general, or some such subject. After supper, though, was the time I liked best. Brandy and my mother would leave for rehearsal and my father and I were alone. Sometimes he'd help me with the piano—he wasn't impatient like my mother was.

My mother was different from most mothers. For one thing, she refused to drive a car. The main difference, however, was her looks. Her eyes and hair were black, and she had a long thin face. When somebody told her once—because of her cheek bones—that her father's upcountry family must have been part Indian, she said they shouldn't worry, she wasn't Indian, more likely part Zulu. No wonder she made people nervous. She was also taller than my father (but then, even I was nearly as tall as my father). Probably the most different thing about her was—she came near to hypnotizing people if she actually talked to them. She seemed to know what a person was thinking—even if she didn't care much about the person.

I *did* love her. I think nobody could quite help loving her in spite of her way of putting people off. (Eventually I began to suspect that her off-putting manner kept people fascinated.) Still, she was a whole lot better on stage than she was at home. She'd studied acting and that meant she had a how-now-brown-cow kind of voice instead of a Charleston voice. Some people said my mother was peculiar in other ways. They said her parents had a mixed marriage, meaning her father came from no-drinking, say-what-you-mean MacIntosh Presbyterians straight out of the red-clay hills of Spartanburg and her mother came from once-upon-a-time low-country Episcopalians, so her insides were at odds with themselves. To me that made no sense. My mother was quite definite about who she was: she was proud of her father's Spartanburg straightforwardness and thought her mother's Charleston deviousness the pit of decadence. So she refused to play bridge or go to tea parties even when she was invited (she was invited, she told me, only because of who her mother was or who my father was.) She preferred to spend her time learning her parts for plays, with Brandy cueing her.

Summers we stayed in the mountains, in Flat Rock. My father couldn't be there much and Brandy tried to make that up to me by packing picnics and playing a lot of badminton. The good thing about the arrangement: Brandy could do the things my father never got around to doing, like fixing lamps and fans and boarding up the house for the winter. It was the Flat Rock Playhouse that took my mother's time.

The summer I was fifteen, Kirk Simons (a tall bookish Charleston boy I liked) was up in Flat Rock for a while. He asked me to climb Hogback Mountain with him—in the dark. The idea, so he said, was to see the sun come up. This kind of thinking of his was one reason I liked him, but I wasn't about to tell Brandy what was up. My mother never much cared what I did but Brandy might decide that climbing Hogback in the dark meant we'd stumble on moonshiners and get shot—and I was going up the mountain with Kirk no matter about getting shot. I decided to simply leave a note and get out of that house quick. I'd slip the note under Brandy's bedroom door.

I woke up in the dark. All the windows in my room were open and the fir trees were scraping the screen and the cool pine smell was making me happy, *and* I had a secret date with Kirk—in the dark, on a mountain top. I felt like gulping the air and running.

Actually I had to tip-toe out my door and step on the boards near the wall that didn't creak. But just as I got to the hall I froze. A form was slipping out of my mother's room and in a flash—long before I could actually see—I knew we were all in hell. I knew it was Brandy naked.

I ducked in my room and laid my head against the wall and didn't move. For a very long time I didn't move. I was feeling sick. I was, in some confused way, thinking: It was *real*. It was *real*—the blackness I'd pressed down. Nobody'd had to know out loud before. Not one soul. Not even me. Now Brandy had seen me. Brandy had seen me seeing her, and I would never be able—ever—not to know again.

That hike up Hogback—for me it was a blackout. I caught myself gasping, and not from heavy climbing. I couldn't think or talk. How was I supposed to go back there? How was I supposed to live?

The only way that made sense was to never go back at all.

By the end of that hike, when I couldn't come up with even a decent-sounding sentence I could say out loud to Kirk, I knew I couldn't speak to anyone. And I had two more years before I could escape to college. Two more years. Until two years were up the world had to stay intact. Just that—stay intact the way I'd pretended it was.

When we got down the stupid mountain I escaped from Kirk. I didn't go back home. I sat in the woods, an hour maybe since I was hungry and then—there they were, Brandy and my mother sitting on the screened porch waiting for me. The way my mother said, "Mary Wright, sit down with us a while," I knew what she meant—those two animal-women meant to draw me in to their abominations. I screamed:

"I hate you. I hate both of you. If either of you tells me a word I'll leave this house for good." Already I was running through the hall and leaping up the stairs.

That did it for my plan to act like I'd always acted. How do you act the same when you're queasy with disgust? No one—no one any time any place—ever—had even heard of a family like mine. I would not stay in this polluted house.

I pulled back from the window when the train lurched into the Charleston station. There was my father on the platform. He was tiny—I hadn't realized before how utterly puny he was. I stared. And I saw what I hadn't expected: my father was not a man. My father was pitiful. How could he have known and just sat there, as if he were almost happy? Why couldn't he see that he hardly existed at all? Why couldn't he see how they'd ground him in the dirt?

I couldn't run up to him like I always had. He was not a father.

Even when we got home and I was alone upstairs at the other end of the house—when I heard him on the piano, the sound gave me the creeps. How could he sit and play music? How could he run his fingers up and down his scales when his house was oozing rot?

He tried to make me say why I was so hateful and miserable, and when I snarled out that this family was too disgusting to exist I could see something sinking in him. At last. He had to know I knew.

At supper, when we were eating at the kitchen table by ourselves, our silence was too creepy for me to bear. I broke it, looking down and not at him. I strained the words out through my teeth: "How could you have let that woman in this house ... for all these years?"

I crouched lower over my plate. No word. It was then—in that wait that might have been forever—I began to feel what I was really doing. I was hoping against hope that I had been mistaken, that in some underground, in some not-admitted way—I was hoping that my father hadn't grasped these things, that my father had no inkling what it was I knew. I was hoping he could be that ignorant—simply because he was a man and men didn't catch these things. My last hope, what I could scarcely dare to hope, was that my good father was still an innocent man.

Only then he answered me. "Sweetpea," he started off, which gave me the heebie-jeebies, along with him speaking more slowly than a dying fly, him saying he'd meant to tell me, saying he'd just been waiting till I was old enough and ready to understand, waiting till I could grasp these very, very complicated things which had never been easy for anybody, ever, to quite know how to treat or talk about.

I bolted as usual. If he thought I would ever be ready to listen, he was mad.

Marna. Maybe Marna could be a tiny patch of relief. It had to be somebody and hadn't she always known?

But when, with her, I attempted to sidle up to the subject, she was more loathsome than before. She wanted every tiny, sickening detail.

That fall Brandy was more or less invisible. And by the time she burst in on our house again we were settled into silent, bitter resentments. I avoided eyes. I'd long given up on Kirk. Now I dropped my piano playing along with dropping my father. My mother lived at rehearsals, so she said. Who cared?

Once at college (in Virginia, but not at my mother's school), I felt as if I'd begun to breathe. But even there, after all this time, it would still come washing over me and send me to bed in the middle of the afternoon, blankets pulled over my head.

In art class I made a new kind of friend, a Jewish girl named Ellie Auslander, a girl with uncontrolled black curls caught in a puff of a ponytail. Ellie was an actual New Yorker, so she liked abstract art. Her room was filled with squares of pure flat black, with tiny misty spots of grey and purple. I wasn't planning to, but late one night I let it out to Ellie. Everything.

Her reaction floored me: Ellie could not comprehend why I was twisting myself in knots. Ellie refused to sympathize. Ellie said that I came from a family of saints—a father who called me *Sweetness*, everybody ("except you") struggling to get along with everybody else. She said nobody chose the kind of persons they could love. Some women loved men, some women loved women, some women—maybe most women—could love both men and women. That was nature, that was the way people were. I was lucky, she said, I was fantastically lucky: my father had not only kept his family but kept his family almost happy and didn't even try to leave Charleston, South Carolina. He was out of this world. He was a Buddha. Was I so blind I couldn't grasp that fact?

I stared. And managed to object. *She* could think this way. She was from New York. She was not from Charleston, South Carolina. What's more, she was wrong about everything being just nature: People *could* decide their lives. People *did*. People had always drawn some line between what was right and what was wrong. People couldn't have a family and keep on living any old way they liked.

At Thanksgiving, at the Charleston depot, my father wasn't waiting for me. Brandy was there, by herself, Brandy announcing my father was in the hospital, but would be all right. My mother had found him this morning. Unconscious. My mother was at Roper Hospital and didn't want anybody there with her—she would call when he came around. People came out of these things, said Brandy. I was to come to her house until my mother called.

I battered her: A heart attack? A stroke? You don't just drop unconscious.

They didn't know yet, she said. But that's not what she meant.

She sat me on her sofa. Her eyes didn't leave me room to get away, so I twisted around to the back of the sofa and dropped my head in my arms. I knew this manner of hers. It meant she was lying. My father was not coming out of this—and wouldn't she be in heaven.

I could not look at her. She waited. I could feel her needing to say something, anything, and after some awkward starts, her voice got a little more regular, though not quite loud enough, and she was on to ancient history, meaning on to the story of my father and my mother and herself. I didn't move or answer but I made sure I heard. I heard her say she was closer to my father than to almost any other person. She said my father was the one who loved my mother the way she loved my mother and neither of them—neither my father nor she herself—could help loving my mother. She said my father had loved my mother since junior high, when they had met in the mountains, at a camp called Kanuga, and finally, in college, she married him. My mother, however, found out that she wasn't cut out for marriage. Yes, she loved me, her baby girl. And she loved my father. But she didn't want to be married—and rather than make my father more miserable than he already was she was going to leave him, bring me to Spartanburg to live with her, and with Brandy. But my father was beside himself. He telephoned Brandy in Spartanburg, said if Brandy would come to Charleston he would find her work and a house and he would welcome her into his home at anytime she wanted. His one request: that she fit into Charleston as smoothly as she could—he practiced law there and so was forced to stay. But he would accept, in his family, what none of them could change. He would adapt. He was capable of that, he said.

Brandy believed him, and Brandy agreed to come. He was an astonishing man, said Brandy—beautiful, surprising, compassionate, taking the cost on himself, and always, always, she'd been conscious of that. He was not small like most men were—he was a huge man—and I must see that. Brandy seemed actually to be begging me.

I opened my eyes. She went on talking but I did not turn around. I was staring out the window, seeing nothing, my blank eyes on Brandy's leather-like, dead hydrangeas. She was making me begin to feel, again, for the man who was my father, who for over two years I'd tried my best to ignore. She was making me remember I and my father had planted these once-white huge hydrangeas when I was a little girl.

Brandy was right. My father had always been the one who had made me happy.

Love is what was disgraceful. Whoever knew what love made people do?

Yet I also knew: it wasn't just Brandy and Ellie who loved him for exactly what he was, it was Charlestonians—it was Missy Van Ness and Mariah Cathcart and even Fanny Heyward—who had seen and *loved* my father for exactly what he was. Charlestonians had never spelled it out in words (that wasn't a habit of theirs). But I grasped—I realized that in some way I had always grasped—what they saw in my father. I recognized it when I'd let myself: my father could keep on loving a woman, keep on and on and on however my mother acted. Charlestonians stood in awe of him, while even now, probably right this minute in his hospital bed, my father was waiting for my mother to look at him.

When that hit me—my father was still waiting—I swallowed even harder and Brandy touched my shoulder. "Mary Wright," Brandy was saying, "he'll come out of this."

I waited. When she didn't go on, I twisted around toward her. Her arms were hugging her chest. Her head was down. After a while she said, low, "Your mother has broken down. She wouldn't look at me. She wouldn't let me anywhere near her."

Oh God, I thought, even now you're bringing things back to your own selfish feelings. You, Brandy, who got us in this mess—you're looking for *my* sympathy?

I said nothing, however, because I realized what her pitiful words could mean—that my mother loved my father. Was there hope?

Brandy's eyes stayed on me, as if she were afraid of me.

I managed an almost sympathetic smile because maybe she—not I—was the left-over one.

She held to her paralyzed kind of fear, holding that expression so long that by the time that she said *suicide* she needn't have bothered to say it. I knew *I* was the one who'd brought this on. My father had turned to me in these last months—more and more in letters I never bothered to answer—and I had turned my back.

I stood up. I announced, "I'm going to the hospital. Will you take me?"

I don't remember Brandy on that drive up Rutledge and across Calhoun. I remember a parade with men on stilts and a Humpty Dumpty hitting our car and me getting lost in long white halls and then my mother's awkward hug—it said they'd pulled him through. I remember my relief. I remember searching out, cautiously, my mother's heavy-lidded eyes to see if I could read what all this meant, and I could not of course. The fear of her was there as strong as ever. Love for her and fear of her, like my father's love and fear, and that stirred up my bleakest suspicion yet: that people never changed. That after this near-death passed by we'd be who we always were. That not one thing in us would know what to do with change—not in my mother and not in my father and not in Brandy and maybe not even in me. This was this and that was that, and what we'd been was what we'd always be.

The thought, oddly, was not all bleak. Or the bleakness was more like stability, like the almost solid, close to accepted, so-long-known-no-longer-audacious, comfortable four of us. ✳

IN WHICH SADIE RUNS OFF TO INDIA TO FIND OUT WHAT THE BIG DEAL IS

> ➤ CHRISTOPHER BUNDY

I dream India because all my mom ever talked about since I was a kid was being there with George Harrison and the Beatles. Like she never did anything else in her life but meditate with rock stars and after that nothing mattered. Let's not even mention me—when she thinks about her wayward daughter, she gets upset, then depressed. The two of us don't exactly qualify as a healthy mother-daughter setup, and when she gets like that, sucked into herself because I lost any one of my stupid part-time jobs or didn't come home for a week straight, I think that's what heavy looks like. So I try not to bother her by staying out of her way mostly, though sometimes we talk and I end up sitting through the same old stories about living in India with the Maharishi. Some joke. This beardy Indian guru scams a bunch of big rich rock stars into going to India. Says he's going to show them the way. The path and the mystery behind transcendental meditation. *TM*, my mom calls it. I saw a thing on *60 Minutes* about people getting sucked in by some baba, though not usually with rock stars but young people like me and Berdy who even went to India to find out for ourselves and had a whole other kind of experience I can't even believe happened anyway. So this oddball Indian shows them a rip-off. Congratulations, you've all been enlightened. Working at the Myrtle Beach National Wax Museum on Ocean Boulevard, my mom doesn't seem so enlightened, even if they do have the entire Last Supper in there.

And of course, there's what happened to Berdy, who had been my boyfriend since junior high school. Another distortion I suspect. But that's fuzzy still, and I'm a little uncertain on what exactly happened. I'm not trying to deny anything, because strange things did happen there that are hard to explain away. Circumstances look bad, and I wouldn't blame anybody for what they thought. But when is anything ever—I mean anything, and I mean ever—just black and just white. Still I dream India.

"Sadie," Berdy said the night we graduated high school, Sadie being my name after a Beatles song, since my mom was so overwhelmed with finding someone to tell her what the hell to do with her life. Berdy looked me in the eye, squinting a little to show me he was serious. "You've been listening to your mother's stories about India since you were a kid. Why don't we just go there and find out for ourselves?"

So we did. From Delhi across to Calcutta, through Rajastan and Gujarat, down to Bombay and farther until we came to a stop in Goa. We went all over that country and still, every time we turned a corner, the place would change and we were overwhelmed all over again. Big country. Not big enough for all those people, but more than some girl from Myrtle Beach, South Carolina, where folks are always coming and going, could ever imagine.

The first I ever saw of India was a photograph mom says my dad took of her somewhere in Kerala, the place of yellow earth and blue sky. I never met him, but my mom says he was all right. *Nothing special, understand,* she says, but not especially bad either, like drunk and cruel or lazy and stupid. He was a gardener, a quiet guy who liked to work with his hands and be by himself. *A smart guy,* she says.

Unfortunately, I think you take after me in the brains department, my mom tells me, always finding new ways to make me feel good.

Mom says my dad didn't like the way people meddled in his life, so he disappeared to a place where they wouldn't bother him. Catch is, my mom never thought to tell him he had a daughter. They weren't tied down by the rules of social or religious order back then, she says. They were more interested in expressing themselves via new freedoms. After she found out she was pregnant with me—one of her new freedoms, I suppose—she packed off in search of another ashram, so she could raise me in this communal atmosphere with lots of mothers and fathers, a whole fellowship of brothers and sisters. She didn't need my dad. It takes a village, I reckon. She had already met the Beatles by this time, which didn't last either. I was too young to remember my time in that giant place, but by the age of six I was already dreaming India. And when I landed there for the second time at eighteen, the rich blue skies of my dreams suddenly made sense to me. As a child, whenever the fan blew or the curtains danced, I dreamed India. As a teenager, when Berdy put his hands on my bare back or grabbed my face to kiss me, I dreamed India. As an adult lost in those sandstorms of drug or alcohol sleep, I dreamed India again. My blue sky. Then Berdy and me went, and I found out for myself. I held Indian earth in my hands and knew I had been there before. It was an uneasy feeling, and I know now I should have listened to the voice inside that said, forget about it. Leave it. There's nothing here for you. Nothing but pain and old mistakes. But I had to find out the hard way.

After I was born, my mother found another ashram in India somewhere in Kerala, where her little experimentation in freedom finally went sour for her and all the other hippies. My best guess is that she, and Berdy later, both went looking for some cockeyed daydream of the counter-culture. A fantasy: a plot of land removed from normal society where they could read to and raise towheaded boys and girls in the embrace of a collective hug, tend their gardens, smoke their pot, and study the teachings of this baba or that. But all they found was dust to dig in and the same anxieties of so-called mainstream society, dishing out responsibilities, breeding tensions, and drawing lines. And the baba, he got himself a half-dozen towheaded girlfriends, pissed off all the guys that were left, and then split with their collective kitty. When I look between the lines of my mom's reminiscences, that's how I see it.

Almost twenty years later, my India wasn't much different. Like I told the Indian police, the consulate lackeys, and anybody else who would listen, what did I know where Berdy had been? We didn't follow each other everywhere. If he wanted to go swimming, he went swimming—he didn't need my permission. But I felt like a bad character with everybody asking me questions. The whole time we were there I never felt real, as if the ground beneath me were swamp, some quicksand reality built on opportunity, psychedelics, and little self-restraint.

And the insanity of India itself does not help. Around us were a few serious freaks, but mostly just kids on long vacations with no one but themselves to answer to. I may sound smart now, but then I could hardly take a step without thrusting my arms forward and feeling my way around on rubber legs, so blind most of the time I gave up on trying to focus, and let the whole place go fuzzy, nothing but vague colors and shapes.

Somehow in the middle of all the carousing and indulgence I pissed Berdy off. Out of my head, of course, way too much *bhang*, and just trying to go with the flow, but Berdy was getting in the way of that and so what? I'm innocent, and I sure as hell didn't make him go in the water. He was so stupid, always acting like he knew everything. For example, on our way to Goa he said we should ride third class. It's cheaper, he said, no big difference. But then he got the time wrong and we got the wrong train, and next thing we're stuck with five million other people, their kids, their sacks and string-bound boxes, their ten thousand smells, and I got my bag ripped open, Walkman, boots, nearly all my shit stolen—and Jesus, Berdy, what the hell were you thinking?

Berdy was always screwing something up. He acted like I didn't matter, as if I wasn't even his girlfriend to watch out for. We got all the way to the train station, and they were herding people on like cattle and Berdy says *over here*, we get on, and the train leaves. We couldn't get to first class because the doors were locked, and we barely found a place to stand. I swear I slept standing up. That's when my pack got ripped, and where was Berdy? Good question. Not watching after me or my pack, that's where. There we were, rolling along, not even on the right train, crammed in with every Hindu in the state heading god-knows-where, and my stuff was walking away faster than I could kick at the little thieves. All that's not important to what happened, but it goes to my point about Berdy screwing things up royal.

I told him, "There are plenty of guys who know how to get things right." I hadn't really pissed him off yet, but Berdy stomped off anyway, leaving me standing in the passageway of this third-class Indian rail car, like I was nobody he knew.

Our second day in Goa—that is when we finally caught the right train and arrived with what was left of our stuff—I went to the beach for a swim. Seems Berdy and I weren't particularly talking much at that point, but I thought maybe he would be there too and see me. I'd let the whole train mess go, and we could get high, watch the sun set, and hold hands as if we still liked each other. Ended up I met this French guy on the beach. Right there things got sore, and I knew why. Again, long story, but let's just say that on this trip of ours, this trip of self-discovery and the like, which I was trying to encourage for both of us, me and French guys—really just one other—had a history of which Berdy was not so fond.

Right off I was flirting with this French guy—on the road being friendly with strangers gets easier—a real hippy-dippy dude dressed in his *tribal*, that's what he called it, *colors*. Claude looked like a clown, barefoot in patchwork pants and vest, scarf around his neck, and long, brown hair pulled up on top of his head in a bun like the goddamned Buddha. He was cute, if a little scruffy, and his voice sexy. Everything he said in that accent sounded deep. Pretty soon he's passing around a joint and the next thing you knew we were both in the ocean, bobbing naked in the water like a couple of seals with the sun sinking behind us. I thought about my mom and how maybe she floated me in these same waters. I was real high, my blue sky going orange as the warmth of the sun spread across Claude's shoulders, his sexy voice floating over the waves to me like a song. It felt like heaven, as if I could breathe water.

"It's the opium." Sexy Claude grinned, his eyes dark hollows.

I wasn't even thinking about Berdy anymore, that shitty fourteen-hour train ride, losing my stuff, or anything but my mom, trying to conjure up this image of the two of us grooving together in the water. There's only one Beatles song I can stand. It's called "Here Comes the Sun," and I swear when you hear it that's all you can think about. It's hard to be depressed when you hear that song. So I got this song in my head—I love it when he sings "little darling ... " like he's talking to me personally—and I imagined my mom singing this smiling song to me and dunking my head in the water, which made me laugh. And I laughed because if you hear my mom talk she doesn't sound like a hippie. She sounds Southern. She also cusses a lot. Nothing serious but *goddamns* and *assholes*—there are lots of *assholes* in the latter parts of my mom's life story. She doesn't even really look much like a hippie anymore, except for her ponytail and some sandals that have seen better days.

Move on, I've been telling her since I was twelve.

What do you know about me? she usually comes back with.

I know you're living in the past, that's what. It's an easy fight and one we've had more times than I care to remember.

So wise for such a screw-up. Okay, I'll give her the occasional screw-up. *No thanks to you.*

I did my best. How many kids get to grow up like you?

Like what? Revolving door dads and some fairy-tales about India. Listen to yourself. I turn it back on her. *Your experiment failed, man.* I can be mean when I want to.

So wise. She'll light a cigarette and return her usual blank stare to the home video show that sometimes gets her laughing or turn the music up real loud. I could easily make her cry here, but I just let it go and move on.

Claude and I didn't do anything in the water but float in a dying orange light, both of us way too high to pull away from such color. Didn't matter to Berdy though. All he saw was the two of us naked in the ocean. Me and Claude. And, like I said, a lot of particulars look bad. Disagreements about my time and place. However you consider what happened, I came out looking bad.

Next thing you knew the police were calling everyone to get out of the water. I thought it was pollution, you know, needles or sewage or something washing up. I really didn't even think about why. In India happenings were always occurring for no apparent reason, and this seemed like one of those happenings. You couldn't fight the chaos or you'd go crazy trying to make sense of it or get an answer from anybody. Claude and I dressed and sat behind a sand dune, the police up the beach getting everybody out of the water. I figured Berdy might be watching me, so I kept flirting with Claude, rubbing up to him, teasing him. I'd show Berdy what he was missing. Before long, Claude was all over me, kissing me. He was sloppy, and kept biting at my lips. I told him it hurt and he'd better be nice to me or I was going to leave. He was no Romeo, and I said I'd go find Berdy. He pushed me down hard in the sand and started pawing at my t-shirt, trying to slide his hands up underneath and telling me nobody was going to find Berdy.

"Riptide," Claude the clown said, his voice not so sexy anymore. "The signs are everywhere."

But I kept expecting to see Berdy come walking up, and then I'd show him. He'd realize he couldn't treat me like shit. There are plenty of other fish around here, I'd tell him. But Berdy didn't show up, and Claude was tugging at my skin like he was pulling taffy. When the police siren went off like any minute fighter planes would nosedive out of the sky, dropping bombs out of their bellies, I was thinking Berdy was probably not going to show up after all. Claude put his hand over my mouth and pushed my head into the sand. All I wanted was to catch Berdy's eye and get a little rise out of him. Then the police were asking me a bunch of questions about why Berdy was in the water by himself and why I was with Claude and were we high on drugs. Claude told them I totally came on to him. It wasn't true, but the police didn't believe me. They wanted to know why I was so mad at Berdy. I swear it's because he forgot so much. He didn't pay attention, so I just wanted to get a rise out of him and show him what he was missing.

In Myrtle Beach again, my blue sky is gone. I still dream India, but it's a cloud of darkness now. I wake up sweating with Berdy's empty eye sockets staring me down, his long hair glistening green like seaweed. His body never turned up, only his day bag and clothes left on the beach, passport, money, and watch all missing when the police found it—*it is regrettable, madam,* the only lame-o answer they could come up with. Since I've been back, my mom has gotten me a job at the wax museum, and we have lunch together every day. She tells me I have to move on and get beyond what happened on the beach in Goa. Nothing I can do will change it. And she reads again from her scrapbook of nostalgia about when things were so much different, so much better. About how she first met George Harrison in Rishikesh, India. How she spent three whole weeks in 1968 meditating with The Beatles under beautiful blue skies. *

EXPECTING GOODNESS

➢ MICHEL S. STONE

Bob and Mimi did not speak on their ride to Dulles, or even after they parked and he covered her with an oversized umbrella when the misting rain began and they waited for the shuttle to the terminal. By the time the shuttle arrived, the mist had turned to rain, heavy and sideways and splashing about their dress shoes. Mimi took the only vacant seat near the front of the crowded shuttle, and Bob moved to the back, finding a seat beside a pale, brunette woman clutching a brown leather purse, a folded newspaper in her lap. The spring morning was already warm, and the shuttle smelled of musty, wet bodies, and popcorn.

Bob had parked in a distant lot and the ride to the terminal would take several minutes. He pulled from his bag a book on woodworking. His grandfather had been a master woodworker, and recently Bob had tried his hand at the craft. His first project had been a candleholder made of walnut, polished smooth, the surface slick, almost silky, and stained dark. He'd given it to Mimi, and she'd called the gift sweet and cute. Next he carved a turkey feather of wood from a linden tree. The material was soft and the blade slipped into it as if it were wax. But lately he'd attempted more ambitious projects, and he'd consulted this book for guidance.

Bob had hoped to finish reading the chapter on table legs today, but after scanning the same sentence three times, he closed the book, and replayed the morning's unresolved argument.

He studied the folks around him, wondering if any of them would be on his flight, a silly thought, really, but one he often had at airports.

The woman beside him appeared to be traveling with her husband and three children. Her children, a teenaged girl and two adolescent boys who might have been twins, looked just like their mother: curly dark hair and wide mouths with slightly protruding teeth. The father and mother had similar facial features, and Bob thought how so many couples begin to favor one another in looks after a while.

His intent, as they had packed their overnight bags that morning, was to be forthright with his wife about his feelings regarding adoption. His timing, he realized now, was where he'd gone wrong. He wanted Mimi to know how he'd always pictured his future, his role as a dad. He wanted her to see what he had always seen: his life revealing itself to him like a flower blooming in time-lapsed photography; he saw it unfolding and he knew what would come next. And then someone pulled the plug on the projector, and the screen went blank. He needed to see the rest of the blooming, the unfolding, and he felt short-changed. Mimi should understand this.

The father of the twins on the shuttle glanced occasionally at the boys but passed the time checking messages on his cell phone. Did the man ever bother to strike up a conversation with his sons?

Even as a teenager Bob had imagined teaching his own future son the art of shooting a layup in basketball, the correct follow-through on a free throw, the skill of catching a pop fly, of scoring a touchdown. He'd show his son how to stick up for himself, how to open the door for a girl, how to shake a man's hand, how to scale a fish. And along with this, he'd teach him the value of integrity and self-respect and honesty. He'd teach him to revere nature, to fly fish, to change a tire, to skip a rock, to mix a bourbon drink.

He thought of his future daughter, too, and all the values he'd instill in her. How lovely she would be! Strong and graceful. Confident and happy. Equipped to tackle all life tossed across her path. Just like her mother.

Now, he found himself heading to Atlanta to meet some young girl whose unborn baby Mimi wanted to adopt. The blooming cherry trees they'd driven past that morning promised springtime's rebirth, but to Bob the blossoms portended the unnaturalness of his potential fatherhood. Some college student in Atlanta had a belly swelling with a baby she wanted to give up, but Bob could not share Mimi's joy over a child with whom he had no genetic link. He had confessed as much at dawn today while he'd packed his duffle.

"Remember when we painted the kitchen," he had said to her. "Remember that was supposed to be fun, a distraction from all the infertility stuff? Well, those paint fumes irritated the hell out of me, Mimi."

Mimi stopped placing clothes in her bag.

"Okay," she said, crossing her arms across her chest and cocking her head to the side in a way that expressed her confusion.

Bob wanted to explain how for him the smell of the paint infiltrated their baby making. How the chemical, almost toxic smell signified to him their mechanical, forced efforts at conceiving. Nothing about the process felt natural or organic, and the painting of the kitchen only proved to be another example of something unnatural and not as it should be. At the time, he'd kept this to himself, not wanting to further distress Mimi, believing stress to be the hindrance to her conceiving.

But the situation evolved, and he'd forgotten about that paint smell until the middle of last night in his agitation, unable to sleep as he considered his diagnosis, for the thousandth time. *Diagnosis.* The word sickened him, connoted a problem, a defect. With his diagnosis came an awareness that part of him was dead; he mourned the child he'd always expected to dream into reality, and the loss broke his heart. His child had always existed somewhere, forming, becoming. How could he explain this to Mimi? She had been disappointed, but not devastated. She had moved on to adoption too easily.

Not until Mimi had undergone several months of infertility treatments with a specialist did the doctor suggest testing Bob, to rule out male infertility. *Sure*, Bob had said. But the process that began as a mere formality resulted in shocking news. Then it was Mimi's turn to be the comforter, the one to say this would work out in God's time, that they had to have faith, and Bob had retreated to his woodworking, cutting out a pattern for a new silver-chest, something lasting and permanent he could give his wife.

As he lay awake last night, reliving the past few years' struggles, he wondered if he never married Mimi, or any woman, would he still be blissfully unaware. He'd been vigorous and spirited in his youth, defying anything to challenge him. Now his youthful optimism had been replaced with a dissatisfaction and an agitation that flowed like sludge through his veins.

So this morning, as Mimi folded her nightgown and Bob said, "I'm not so sure about raising a child that doesn't come from us," his comment blindsided her, and he knew it. He should have said this months earlier. She told him as much, shouted the words, just before she shut down altogether and become silent on their drive to Dulles.

He watched Mimi now chatting with an elderly woman sitting beside her on the shuttle, but Bob could not hear their voices over the din of the shuttle's engine. The teenage daughter of the woman beside Bob read a paperback edition of *Jane Eyre* and the twins played hand-held video games and shared a large bag of popcorn, the source of the smell Bob had sensed upon boarding. He studied the features of the travelers on the shuttle and wondered what the pregnant coed whom he and Mimi would meet in Atlanta that afternoon would be like.

When the woman next to Bob turned to him and said, "Do you have children?" the sad look in her eyes surprised him. This woman's eyes were dark and cold, like raisins set in raw dough, and they held no gleam hinting at the joys and challenges of parenthood. Her cheek-bones sat high in her skull, and she might have been attractive years earlier.

"No," Bob answered. "Not yet, anyway." He lowered his gaze and noticed the woman's thin, pale hands tremble in her lap.

The woman turned away, looking toward her children, watching the boys play and the girl read and the husband push buttons on his cell phone.

Sometimes, Bob considered soldiers, who for months after losing limbs in war complained of phantom pains, of spikes being driven into hands that weren't there, of ghost-feet that throbbed, and he under-stood how something nonexistent could cause pain.

He looked at the woman's daughter, just a few years younger than the girl he and Mimi would soon meet in Atlanta. He recalled his comments to Mimi as they'd backed out of the driveway on their way to the airport, his attempt to voice his reservations.

"What do we know about this girl, Mimi?" he had said. "Some college kid who made a poor choice one night at a frat house. How many other bad choices has she made before this?"

"What are you talking about? Her poor choice?" Mimi said. "I'm focused on her wise judgment to give up a child she's unprepared for."

"I'm just saying she'll have a history we can't possibly know," he said.

"And that matters to you, why?" she'd asked.

"A thousand reasons, Mimi."

She raised her eyebrows, waiting.

"You can nurture a bad seed all you want, but it won't bear decent fruit," he said.

She wrinkled her brow. "Are you talking about yourself?"

Bob froze, stunned by her audacity, her malicious effort at wit. But as she stared at him, her hands spread wide in the air before her, he realized her intent was not sarcasm. Mimi was perplexed; she truly did not get his point.

"Love's important, but sometimes genetics win," he said.

"And sometimes, Bob, loving parents with no history of anything toxic raise imperfect children. That's called life," she'd shouted.

Now, Bob opened the book in his lap but immediately closed it. Wishing he could concentrate, he considered some of the pieces he'd made Mimi: the silver chest he'd lined with purplish felt, the quilt rack, the jewelry box with delicate, intricate inlay. He believed each piece to be more beautiful and unique than the one before it, and relished the creation of tangible, long-lasting objects sprung from his mind and his hands, his ideas made concrete. Presenting these objects to Mimi gave him great pleasure.

He slipped the book into his bag, too distracted to read.

When the stranger beside Bob turned to him again, she spoke so softly Bob was unsure if he heard her correctly.

"Pardon?" Bob said, noticing she'd wrapped her fingers around the newspaper as if to steady them.

"I know this sounds strange," she said, dropping the paper to her lap and intertwining her fingers. "I have cancer." She stared at her clenched hands then looked up, met his gaze, and said, "Pancreatic." Her lips, like her fingers, were thin, pale, and dry.

"Oh," Bob said. "I'm sorry." In an instant, he doubted her, wondered if she was a crazy person, and he fought the urge to move away from her. Then, just as quickly as he had doubted her, he believed her. Her eyes told him the truth.

"They don't know," she said, nodding toward her family.

Bob followed her gaze. "I imagine telling your kids such news is hard," he said. Just then the woman's boys, laughing, slapped a high five in response to the video game they played.

She nodded. "I haven't told my husband, either. I haven't told anyone." She lowered her voice as if ashamed and said, "I don't know how."

The shuttle closed in around them, shrunk to a capsule. No one was there, not even Mimi, and the musty air grew stifling, the popcorn odor nauseating, and the drone of the engine screamed at him.

"Oh, man," he said, at once embarrassed at the sound of his words, puny and insufficient.

"I just got the diagnosis yesterday morning. I just ... It's just ... We've had this trip planned for so long." She sniffled and looked away, rubbing her left thumb over and over again against her right palm as if trying to remove a stain, and said nothing else.

When the shuttle stopped at the first terminal, the family gathered their bags and exited. The woman did not turn to look at Bob. Her husband's eyes met Bob's, and he acknowledged Bob with a slight departing nod, the way polite strangers do when they are going their separate ways. Bob wanted the woman to acknowledge him with a glance, so he could offer her a smile or a look that might say, *I really am so sorry.* He watched the woman and her family through the window until the shuttle lurched and pulled away from the curb.

He admired the family resemblance among them and ached knowing he'd likely never have that with offspring of his own. If he and Mimi adopted the child in Atlanta, then years from now, strangers would look at them and not see a family resemblance. This knowledge saddened him, and self-loathing festered in him for his inane shallowness.

He'd heard of such things, of people making confessions to strangers when they couldn't say the words to the ones who mattered most, though he had never before had such an experience.

He wished he'd told the woman he'd say a prayer for her health and for her ability to tell her family. Instead, he'd watched her gather her bags and her family and go, and his passivity further unsettled him.

The old woman beside Mimi had gotten off the bus, and Mimi sat alone, her eyes closed, head back, resting. Did she imagine the fetus, its cells dividing wildly inside another woman's womb in Atlanta? Or did Mimi consider Bob at that moment? Could she somehow comprehend his recoiling from this adoption? Could she understand that if Bob accepted that option and agreed to it, his diagnosis would become a reality, that he'd be accepting the doctor's conclusion? Did she understand how badly he wanted their child to be *their child*, not some stranger's?

At the ticket counter, Bob slipped his hand around Mimi's, threading his fingers with hers.

"I want to trust that the world is good. Do you know that?" he said.

She lifted her sunglasses from her face so that he could see her eyes. They were beautiful eyes, warm and vibrant and hopeful, eyes that expected the world to be decent and right.

He wondered at her optimism and her faith, even after all the years of disappointment.

Leaning in close to his face, she whispered, "I know that, and I wouldn't want to raise a child or face the risks of this adventure with anyone but you."

Bob considered his wife's words. *Risk. Adventure. Anyone but you.*

He fingered the book wedged in the bag across his shoulder. Perhaps on the plane he'd take a look at the chapter on cradles.

The man behind the ticket counter shouted "next" and Bob and Mimi moved forward. *

THE NIPPER

> SUSAN TEKULVE

— — — — — — — — — — — —

In early February, still winter in the coal camp, the road leading from his grandparents' frame house to the mine stretches before Dean like a white lake. Because he is fourteen and small for his age, Dean's Grandpa Santorelli and Uncle Carlo must carry him through the high, spring snow. When his grandfather tires, his uncle lifts Dean onto his shoulders. In the pre-dawn darkness, Dean feels his uncle's stout chest heaving beneath his calves, his hobnail boots slicing right through the snow, his heels thumping hard against the frozen earth. Uncle Carlo's tobacco breath floats upward, clouding the gray icy air. This manly smell comforts Dean as they approach the black coal-crusher hulking over the colliery.

At the bath house, his grandfather and uncle strip off their street clothes, place them in metal baskets, and pull them up to the ceiling, where they hang limply from hooks among hundreds of empty white shirts. After dressing, Carlo goes down to the stables to curry comb his mule and check the fit of her harness while Grandpa Santorelli takes Dean to the gangway and shows him the heavy, wooden door built across the tunnel opening.

"Inside the door, there is a giant fan that pulls fresh air into the mine," his grandfather explains. When the door is closed, the air hits it, turning back into the underground tunnels and chambers where the miners work, keeping deadly gasses from building in pockets, pushing out the black damp. For the next twelve hours, Dean must keep the door shut so that the good air remains inside, opening it only to let full cars out into the coal yard and empty ones back in.

Grandpa Santorelli shows Dean how to how to handle the door when a mine car approaches, how to pour water over the carbide to light his lamp. Then, suddenly, he blows out the flame, showing Dean just how dark it can get beneath the earth, telling him how this solitary job as the nipper will breed the courage he'll need to become a miner some day. The flint snaps again, and his grandfather's face reappears in the blue lamp light, warning Dean that he must never fall asleep.

"How do I stay awake?" Dean asks.

"Play with the rats." His grandfather turns, walking down the gangway to the mine trip car. His lamp light flutters like a yellow bird, casting shadows against the tunnel walls. "Share your lunch with them. Keep them close, and they will tell you when the roof is working."

When the mine trip car disappears around the first bend of the tunnel, Dean shuts the door and sits on his bench beside a pile of shale, putting his carbide lamp beside him. In the sudden, heavy silence, he wonders, *How does a roof work?* But he hears only an occasional pick axe from a nearby chamber, a rat scuttling across the floor. It stands on its hind legs in front of Dean, and begs like a squirrel.

"You ain't no squirrel," Deans says, tossing a piece of shale at it.

The rat whips its naked tail at Dean's lunch pail, knocks off the lid. Dean pulls his lunch closer, checks on his ham biscuits and beans while the rat slips back into a hole in the wall, its fat belly and fur dragging across the dirt floor. Dean hates rats. Playing with a rat, he thinks, would betray the memory of his father, a railroad man who called coal operators "sewer rats" and never worked in the mines. Once, an army of real rats infested an abandoned dairy below the mountain farmhouse where Dean and his parents had lived. For a month, Dean's father came home after a day of grading Tidewater coal at the station, and sat in the open kitchen window, shooting off the rats as they marched up the sloping ridge below their house, the same ridge tramps wandered over, glassy-eyed from whatever they drank from their paper sacks, asking his father for money, sometimes work.

"You're like tramp bait," Dean's mother had told his father, claiming a tramp could find his father among a crowd of one hundred. Though his father rarely had cash money or work to give, he always offered each tramp a boiled egg, or some rhubarb jam on biscuits. Dean's mother worried over his father's habit of feeding the tramps, but his father claimed they were harmless, just hungry. Then one February night a tramp shot him dead by the train tracks, stole his railroad watch, hopped back onto the train, and was never seen again.

The day after his father was buried, Dean's mother climbed into her big brass bed, pulled her ivory wedding ring quilt up to her chin. Dry eyed, neither awake nor dreaming, she stayed in the bed with her angry, grieving face turned to the wall while Grandmother Santorelli explained that she was taking Dean back with her to the coal camp in War, West Virginia, until his mother could "get herself straight." Though Dean was too young to work underground, his grandmother paid the foreman twenty-five cents for an age blank, passed Dean off as a small fourteen-year-old so that he could be the nipper.

Now, as he sits in the mine gangway, Dean ponders how he should play with the rats and stay awake. Trying to think up a rat game, he looks around the chamber, finds an empty powder tin, and baits a piece of wire with a slice of ham biscuit. Placing the wired ham biscuit inside the tin, he sets the trap on the floor across the coal car track, laying a sheet of paper over the tin's opening, holding the other end of the wire that will slam the heavy powder lid over the rat.

A rat crawls out of its hole, sniffs the air around Dean's trap, slips inside. Dean pulls the wire, slamming the lid over the tin, running to clasp the lid in place. Holding the jerking can in his arms, Dean listens to the angry keen of the rat, unsure of what to do now that he's caught it. His carbide lamp flickers weakly. He's afraid that if he sets the angry rat free, it will turn on him and bite. *This ain't play,* Dean thinks. Truth is, the only game Dean wants to play is poker.

The previous Sunday, Grandpa Santorelli took him to eat supper at the boarding house that his mother's favorite aunt, Maria, runs for single miners. Short and plump, Maria smells of dirty dishwater and the cigars she smokes when she sits in her aluminum rocker on the back porch every day. All through the meal, she stood at the head of a long picnic table in the dining room, between the pictures of a crucified Jesus and Henry Ford that hung on the wall behind her bench. Serving macaroni and tomato sauce from a bone china bowl, she passed around tough bread, seasoned with the bitter herbs she found in the woods, ordering all the men to eat with a "*Prego. Prego.*" When the pasta bowl was empty, the men moved outside to gamble on the back porch. Hands wrapped around water glasses filled with young wine, they bet each other on who could eat the hottest pepper each had grown that summer. They bet on hand after hand of stud poker, five card or seven. They bet on who could tell the dirtiest joke.

While the men gambled on the porch, Dean helped Maria clear and wash the dishes. Despite his great aunt's dishwater smell and fearsome table manners, Dean understood why his mother loved her. Maria wore a faded silk yellow dress beneath her stained apron, and gold hoop earrings. Her round face remained smooth, her brown eyes wide and innocent, even though his mother said she'd once run off with a miner who left her for dead in Detroit, and Lord knows what kind of trouble she got into before she appeared back in the camp and took over the boarding house for her parents. That was thirty years ago, and Maria's siren beauty and flight to Detroit were only one of his mother's bedtime stories. Now, Maria kept a deck of playing cards in her apron pocket, and after she wiped down the picnic table, Maria dealt a hand of poker to anyone who'd sit across the picnic table from her. Too young to play cards with the men on the porch, Dean gladly accepted the cards that his aunt dealt swiftly and deftly with her fortune-teller hands.

"What do you wanna play poker for?" his aunt asked.

"Money," he said. "You can make hundreds of dollars if you're good at it."

"You gonna buy a mule like your Uncle Carlo?"

"I got other plans," he said.

"Good," she said. "Mules are more expensive than men and twice as hard to keep. Now Carlo, he is a little pazzo about his mule." She circled her finger near her head and rolled her eyes. "That mule gives him three broken ribs, but he treats her like a sweetheart."

Dean laughed. "He calls her Peaches."

Maria studied him. "Those men on the porch aren't real poker players. They are gamblers."

"What's the difference?"

"A gambler bets a hundred dollars on what he has in his hand. A poker player bets on what he thinks the other players have."

"How do you know so much about gamblers and poker?"

"I was married to a gambler who worked as a sweeper in the Ford plant," she said. " I became a poker player to get back home after he left me in Detroit."

"I'm sorry." Dean waited, hoping she'd give him the parts of the story that his mother never told him, but Maria only patted his hand. "It was long ago. *C'era una volta.*"

The powder can jerks in Dean's arms. His fingers have fallen asleep from holding down the lid, and he can't remember why he decided to catch the rat in the first place. He knows only that a rat is too dumb to play poker. Even if it had the brains for a hand of five card draw, this one would probably cheat. When a coal cart rumbles to the door, Dean clenches his rat trap shut with his left hand and opens the mine door with his right to let his Uncle Carlo drive his mule through. Standing on the front car bumper, his braided whip curling from his belt, Carlo guides his mule by voice, speaking softly in Italian, "*Vai*" and "*Va bene*," until the mule steps into the gangway. Dean closes the door, holding tightly to the tin can.

"What have you got in the can?" his uncle asks.

Dean shrugs, feeling foolish, and the can nearly jerks out of his arms. "A rat," he says.

Carlo looks from the can to Dean's face, but he doesn't laugh. "Why did you put a rat in the can?"

Dean flushes. "Grandpa Santorelli told me to play with the rats so I could pass the time and stay awake. I caught this one, but now I can't figure out how to let it go without getting bit."

Carlo dismounts his coal car, squeezes past his thick, swaggering mule. He places one hand on the lid of the can, the other on the bottom. Setting the can down on the other side of the track, he backs away. The angry rat bursts from the can, screeching and lurching toward his uncle. Carlo cracks his black whip above the rat's head, and the rat scuttles behind the pile of shale.

"A mule would make a better pet," Carlo says, pulling sugar cubes out of his pocket, offering them to his mule on his flattened palm. "My Peaches knows her way through these tunnels without looking. If I get lost, I just unharness her and follow her to the surface."

"Is she blind?"

"No. During the strike a year ago, all the mules were brought up to the surface. They trembled in the sunlight, but not one of them was blind. Peaches was hard to get out of the pasture and back into the mine. I think she has been a little bit angry about it ever since."

Carlo pulls two boiled eggs, two sausages, and two fried apple pies from his pocket, feeding one of the eggs, a sausage, and a pie to his mule, eating the rest after his mule is fed. "You want to hear another secret?"

Dean nods.

"It's Peaches' birthday today. That is why I give her the pie with her sandwich."

"How do you know it's her birthday?"

"Because it is my birthday, and I bought her on this day four years ago. Now, we are like *gemelli*," he pauses, searching for the word in English. "We are ... like twins."

"Well, happy birthday to you both, I guess."

Dean studies his uncle's mule. Her long ears have been filed down by the low mine ceilings, her wiry coat singed from her back during a long-ago mine fire. When Dean moves a little closer, Peaches tries to nibble Dean's flannel shirt right off his back. He suspects that the mule is at least ten years older than his uncle, who at eighteen is the best and oldest mule driver in the mine. Still, the mule is short, stocky and dark, like his uncle; she favors Carlo the way a pampered dog will come to look like its faithful owner.

"What time is it?" Dean asks.

Carlo shrugs. "The foreman took my watch away when I became a driver so that I would think only about the number of cars."

"How do you know when to quit?"

"All I need to know is that I have six more chambers to get to before I can go home. I stay until the work is done."

"Aren't you ever afraid of being alone after the other men leave?"

Carlo laughs. "You are just a boy, but you talk like a very old man. Peaches takes me through tunnels where the foreman never goes. I prefer that to sitting all day in the gangway, or hunching over like a monkey in a hole. For me, the work is freedom. It is like paradise."

Carlo stands, brushes his lunch crumbs from his coveralls, squeezes past his mule. When his mule refuses to budge, Carlo cracks his whip in the air above her head, coaxing, "*andiamo*," and the cart moves slowly toward the end of the tunnel, toward white sunlight. Sitting back on his bench, Dean imagines Carlo twisting and turning through miles of the deepest mine tunnels, oblivious to time, as carefree and graceful as a man on a holiday sleigh ride. Dean envies his young uncle's freedom, his courage. Most of all, he envies Carlo's lunch, which was packed by Aunt Maria, who treats Carlo like her own son.

The scent of fried apple pie lingers in the gangway. Dean's stomach tugs with hunger until he remembers his own lunch, packed by his grandmother, a tall, blond woman who came down from Ohio to teach in the company school and stayed after she married Dean's Italian grandfather. She makes Dean sleep on the bed tick behind the coal stove in her kitchen, his mother's cramped childhood bed. His grandmother's country ham tastes like sweat and salt, and the dry biscuit crumbles when he lifts the sandwich to his mouth.

The dark gangway smells like the inside of Dean's mother's oven, and he longs to be in his mother's kitchen on a Sunday morning when, off from the railroad, his father always planned supper while his mother was still washing the breakfast dishes. The yellow kitchen was warm and narrow, but Dean lingered at the round trundle table, watching his father cook with his mother. Hands moist with dishwater, his mother peeled potatoes and carrots while his father dredged strips of wild rabbit in flour and mustard, wrapping the winter vegetables and rabbit inside a buttery pie crust. His father gently touched the small of his mother's back when he reached around her for the salt and pepper; she arched her spine absentmindedly to let his arm pass. Now, as he sits in the cold gangway, looking down at the loveless, watery beans in his lunch, Dean thinks of his father's cooking as a graceful dance by a man who never grew old or bitter enough to hate food and his own family.

Dean forces a biscuit down, and it sits like a stone in his stomach, cramping his left side. He sets his carbide lamp on the floor and lies down on his bench, kneading the cramp with his left hand. When the cramp loosens, he grows dangerously sleepy. He stands, taking a deck of cards from his coverall pocket. Though she hadn't packed a lunch for him, his Aunt Maria gave him a deck of cards before he left the boarding house last Sunday, taught him a makeshift game—a cross between five-card draw, solitaire, and a carnival penny toss—that would amuse him and keep him awake while he waited and worked the heavy gangway door all day.

Kneeling, Dean deals the cards face up on the dirt floor, seven cards to a row, until he's dealt out the whole deck. He digs five small pieces of coal from the wall with his thumbnail and tosses them one by one at the cards before him. Leaning over, he reads the cards where the coal chips have landed by the blue lamplight. During the first few hands, the coal chips land on a pair of jacks, a three of a kind and a flush. When he hears a car rumbling toward the door, he picks up the cards and opens the door. Closing the door after the car passes, he reshuffles the cards, deals another hand on the floor, tossing the coal chips towards the cards that lie beyond him in the darkness.

Time passes. Thinking only of cards and the mine door, he is no longer bored or lonely or afraid. Just as he begins to believe that he might just master the darkness and solitude, he deals a hand, tosses the coal and walks over to the cards, slowly reading the ten, jack, king, queen and ace of spades, each lying beneath a coal chip. Heart pounding, Dean recalls sitting across the picnic table from his Aunt Maria, her dark hands folded around his hand, warning. *There's always a chance of a royal flush. It only happens once, if it happens at all. One day, if you get one, you'll wish you'd been playing for cash money.* Stomach sinking, Dean knows he's gotten his only royal flush, that he's spent it on the floor of a mine, in his own penniless company.

"What are you doing?" His grandfather stands over him, looking puzzled at the scattered cards on the mine floor. Dean follows his grandfather's gaze to the gangway door, which must have swung open sometime between the last coal car and his discovery of the royal flush. His grandfather's pained and worried eyes aren't blaming. Still, the shame and fear washes over Dean so suddenly that his skin burns with it.

"Where's Carlo?" his grandfather asks.

"I saw him a little while ago at lunch time."

"It's six o'clock. All the other drivers have gone home."

Dean's hand moves to his left forearm, toward the promise of his father's watch, finds only his naked, bony wrist. He looks toward the drift mouth, at the dark hole where daylight had flickered across the melting patches of snow the last time he looked. His grandfather turns, stooped and weary this time, heading back down the gangway. When Dean asks if the other miners will help search, his grandfather explains that you got paid for removing coal from the mines, not the pieces of another man's crushed and buried body.

"This is the bad work," his grandfather says. "Go home and tell your grandmother that I'll be late."

Dean ignores his grandfather's command, following him, and his grandfather doesn't resist. Down and deeper into the drift mine, the tunnel narrows, and they pass abandoned coal seams, some dry, some sinking beneath a foot of water, all of them cut between stripped timbers that squeeze beneath the mine roof. Dean's stomach clenches from the narrow tunnels, from the thought that he and his grandfather are completely alone, and Carlo could be miles away, trapped beneath a roof fall, passed out from invisible gas that could have crept through the tunnels while Dean was playing cards in the gangway. As they approach the deepest level of the mine, where the mules are kept in stables cut into rock, a stream of rats rushes past them, heading up and out of the mine.

At the stable door, Dean hears his uncle singing, *Happy birthday to me. Happy birthday to you.* Inside, the stable smells of old manure and straw and his Aunt Maria's fried apple pie, and Carlo sits western style on Peaches in front of the other mules that are already put up in their stone stalls, their rope halters hanging from pegs nailed into the mine ribs. Carlos wears a pointed birthday hat on his head; another sits between his mule's ears. Dean nearly cries with relief to see his crazy, living uncle, still in one piece, singing a drunken birthday song, his terrible voice chasing the rats from the stables. Moving closer, he sees that his uncle is not drunk. Carlo's eyes are glassy, but no bottle is in sight. The other pit mules sway and stamp in their stalls, their eyes wild, their thick necks straining toward the open doorway. Peaches stamps her hooves, looking ready to kick three more of Carlo's ribs and charge out after the rats, but Carlo hangs on, finishing his strange serenade, *Happy birthday dear me and Peaches. Happy birthday to me and you.* His grandfather shakes his head slowly, saying, "It is the gas."

Uncle Carlo passes out, his body sliding off the mule, but Dean's grandfather catches Carlo before the frantic mule can stomp him into the ground. He lays Carlo on a mine plank, forming a makeshift litter that the mule can drag out of the mine behind her. Then he ties his handkerchief over Dean's nose and mouth, motioning for Dean to hand him the rope halter hanging on the peg beside him. As his grandfather begins to lash the end of the plank to the mule's belly, the mule sways violently, squeezing him into the wall. His grandfather stumbles, hitting his head on a coal seam, the breeze of his falling body snuffing out the carbide lamp.

Alone, in the complete darkness that was supposed to make him adult and brave, Dean wants to flee, following the rats toward the surface. Though he can't see them, he feels the rats climbing over the still bodies of his grandfather and uncle. He recalls standing at the head of his father's casket, feeling his father's weight shift as he helped lift the coffin into the black wagon, knowing his father's face was directly beneath his fingertips. The truth of his father's death settles over him like the mountain's deadly weight, pushing down, squeezing the breath out of him. He knows that if his father were alive, he would tell Dean that manhood isn't about cutting your losses, planning your own elaborate escapes.

Reaching down, Dean finds his grandfather and pulls him on top of his uncle on the plank, stacking the men as though readying them for a long, upward sleigh ride. Guided by touch and sound, he lets the other pit mules out of their stalls one at a time, allowing them to lead the way toward the surface. He strokes Carlos' mule on her flank, calming her enough to remove her harness. He follows the mules up through the tunnel, toward open air and safety, steadying the plank that holds his uncle and grandfather.

At the drift mouth, Dean is met by a group of the single Italian miners who played cards on his Aunt Maria's porch last Sunday. After listening for Dean's grandfather and uncle's breathing, they load the two still-unconscious men into a horse-drawn wagon and take them back to Aunt Maria's boarding house. Later, the mine inspector will say that the stable air was impure enough to make a grown man fall, but it had not been as deadly as the black damp. Now, at this odd hour, the breaker whistle blows, and the streets jam with miners' wives spilling from tarpaper shacks, walking toward the colliery, their faces tilted shyly toward disaster. Dean already knows the crisis has been averted, that he has in fact saved twenty pit mules that are worth twice as much as his uncle and grandfather in the eyes of the foreman, but he walks unnoticed against the steady stream of women, away from the colliery, dodging dirty, melted piles of snow along the road that stretched out before him that morning, white and pristine in the blue, dawning light.

Following the train track down to his Aunt Maria's house, he sees an Italian boy sitting on the rickety back steps of a tarpaper shack. The boy is wrapping string around a rubber ball, covering it with black electrical tape. He throws the makeshift baseball against an empty coal car, running to field it. When the baseball lands at Dean's feet, he pauses, staring hard into the boy's familiar face, but he cannot recognize him. He steps over the ball and hands the boy his deck of cards. He keeps walking until the breaker whistle sounds, like a tired voice in the distance. ✴

ICE

I would never have believed that I'd break my pelvis falling off the roof, because I could not have pictured myself on the roof in the first place. In the seventeen years I'd lived in the house, I'd never gone up there and I could not have imagined any circumstances that would get me there. Hell, I paid a teenager in the neighborhood an outrageous sum to clean the gutters, just so I wouldn't have to climb up where a man of my limited agility should not be.

The ice storm left over a million people in the Southeast without power. It littered a good chunk of four states with fallen tree limbs, which fractured roofs and crushed fences, dented hoods, and smashed windshields. My own upstate South Carolina neighborhood was part of the wasteland, our eighty-year-old oaks snapping in the night with rifle-like smartness that sent my German Shepherd into whiny, pacing fits in the hall. At one point I was awakened by a crash that sounded as if an entire tree were coming through the ceiling. It *was* an entire tree, up by the roots, but it only grazed the side of the house, one of its branches grabbing and ripping the gutter away like a pull-tab from a box top.

The next morning I was eating cereal in front of the TV in the den. I did so out of habit; the TV was not on. We'd lost power at some time in the night. An occasional snap and crash of a tree limb could still be heard outside. Cassie shuffled into the den, dressed in her furry slippers and robe.

"A man in our yard is hauling limbs to the street," she said.

"Who is he?" I asked.

She shrugged. "Beats me. He's pretty big, whoever he is."

I put my cereal bowl down on the coffee table and rose from the couch. My knees made popping sounds like the breaking trees when I stood. By the time I reached the living room and looked out the front window, no one was in sight. Several large tree limbs were stacked neatly by the side of the road.

"Maybe he'll come back and do the backyard," Cassie said, from over my left shoulder. I hadn't heard her come in the room. We had recently become accustomed to ignoring each other, and this simple, mutual look out the window was an uncomfortable closeness.

Only a week earlier Cassie had mentioned the possibility of a trial separation. She'd said it casually, as if contemplating a new hairstyle or the prospect of taking up a new hobby. We'd both become experts at malicious nonchalance, at taking the emotion out of our voices so that the *doesn't-really-matter-to-me* of our words would make them sting more. But I knew I was better at it than she was.

"It's either that or marriage counseling," she announced, raising the stakes. She knew that being forced to consider the mediation of an outsider would offend my stubborn sense of independence.

But I held my own and said nothing, only looked up from my computer Solitaire game, nodded dismissively, and went back to playing.

She sighed and threw up her arms.

Silence and blankness of body language: the ultimate in nonchalance. I'd learned early in our marriage to use reticence as a weapon when I felt confronted, and by now it was a physiological response. Or non-response, to be accurate. The perfect opposite of Fight or Flight, Do Nothing had shielded me from confrontation for most of my marriage. I avoided conflict the way I avoided climbing on my roof. During our rare arguments, Cassie had always pointed out that to avoid conflict was sometimes to avoid responsibility as well, but I could dismiss this notion too, once she threw up her arms in surrender, which she always did.

The truth is, I was taken aback, even if I didn't show it. Since Jannie, our only daughter, had gone off to college, I'd thought Cassie and I would continue ignoring the void in our relationship. It had always been so easy to overlook marital shortcomings when we were in the throes of childrearing. And Jannie was such an energetic and talkative child that she pretty much shouldered the household duties of conversation and personal interaction for eighteen years. I just assumed Cassie and I would accept our lack of responsiveness to each other, now that it had become so apparent, and coast into old age on security and complacency. The thought of coasting alone had not seriously occurred to me. But superficial stoicism notwithstanding, the thought of losing Cassie scared the hell out of me.

Neither of us mentioned the side yard, where the whole tree had fallen, tugging up a big clump of red dirt and gnarled roots like giant arthritic fingers stubbornly refusing to give up life. It was a job bigger than we were and we'd need the help of a professional.

The backyard, on the other hand, seemed to be a disaster zone we could slowly clear ourselves. We would probably get someone to repair the chain link fence, which was smashed in two places, but the cleanup we would do on our own. We had six oaks on about half an acre back there, and each tree looked to have lost a couple of major limbs and countless smaller ones. You could barely see the ground for all the timber. The iced spots that were visible shone like silver, mysterious coins from a lost civilization. Nothing in the scene was familiar. Even the shrubbery lining the glazed chain-link fence looked foreign, the barren branches encased in ice and bent dolefully to the ground.

"I'll walk down to Jeff's and borrow his chainsaw," I said. "Why don't you call the insurance company?"

"The phone's dead," she said, with a tone of impatience.

Jannie had come home for Christmas, just weeks before the ice storm. She'd come on the twenty-third with her boyfriend, Rex, who dressed neatly in wool sweaters and khaki pants, was fawningly polite, and talked of future plans that included law school and sailing trips, missions to build orphanages in third world countries. Kids these days, I swear. They think they can do anything.

On Christmas day we opened presents, ate cinnamon buns, and drank hazelnut coffee all morning, as if we needed a sugar and caffeine buzz to last us for life. In the afternoon we had turkey sandwiches and beer. We played Scrabble and Twister. Cassie and I laughed more than we had in a long time, but when our eyes met in mid-laugh, we both turned to Jannie, either too afraid or too resentful to enjoy a laugh with each other.

The next morning Jannie and Rex left for Florida, where their college team was playing in a bowl game. A cold rain fell as we waved goodbye from the driveway until they were completely out of sight.

"How about some Scrabble?" I said to Cassie, about an hour after they'd gone.

"Don't," she said, and I knew she was right. We couldn't pretend that we didn't both ache with loneliness, that we weren't depressed by the realization that from now on, Jannie would be increasingly more visitor than resident, and all we really had for most of the days' long domestic hours was each other, which didn't seem like much.

When I walked outside I looked in the street where among the branches and ice lay a lumpy gray mass that I assumed was road kill, but upon closer inspection proved to be a stuffed donkey. Some child's lost Eeyore, I supposed. I kicked it to the side of the street, where it rested on the curb right beside the pile of branches the mysterious man had stacked. Looking back at the house I noticed that we had a big limb hanging on a wire that ran parallel to, and directly over, the peak of the roof.

Cassie's brother, Jeff, lived less than a mile away, on a large lot with a lawn so lush it could have been green velvet, with only a couple of dogwoods and a small Japanese maple for trees. I don't know why he had a chainsaw. He had a shed full of power tools he never used.

Ours was an old neighborhood with houses from the days of big rooms, high ceilings, and superior craftsmanship. There were Dutch colonials and bungalows, a few huge Victorians. Jeff was at the very edge of our neighborhood, near a more modern area. His property had been an empty lot until he bought it and built his two-story brick house. Walking down there I passed dark, old, icy house after dark, old, icy house where my neighbors lived, people who in the summer sat on their front porches and read library books while their kids played or sold lemonade in the front yard. It could seem so Mayberry at times, though now no one was out, and the whole place was desolate and unfriendly. The occasional sound of a limb falling, and the more frequent crashes of ice sliding off of roofs, seemed like threats from the Old Testament God.

I thought of when we first moved in, when Jannie was a baby, how we'd had countless barbecues and front porch sing-alongs with neighbors, many of whom had young kids too. Some of those people were gone now, and most of the ones still around kept to themselves much more than they used to. I understood. I kept more to myself, too. I didn't think any of us could really explain our transformation into recluses, but I sensed that we'd all, perhaps to varying degrees, accepted it as the natural course of life. As our energy levels waned, our need for social interaction became relatively less important.

A limb cracked and fell in the yard I was walking past. Not a very big one, but it made enough noise to startle me. In the road I thought I was more or less safe, though some trees did overhang the street. I looked up and didn't see any limbs that could fall on me, so I continued.

It wasn't as if anything major had happened with Cassie and me—nothing explosive. But every day since Jannie had gone had been a non-event, and the emptiness left us much room to implode. We'd both lived for Jannie's visits, from the day we left her in her dorm, though the visits were infrequent now that she'd found a boyfriend, and we knew they'd become even more infrequent as the years passed. Cassie talked forever with Jannie on the phone. I wasn't much of a phone person, but I wrote my darling daughter lots of emails. If Cassie and I were to split up, I wondered whom Jannie would visit more.

Of course this wasn't the only thing I wondered. I also wondered what I would do with all the other hours, the overwhelming majority of time I'd spend at home alone if Cass were really gone.

Jeff's lawn was hardly its normal verdant self. He did have a winter grass—light green with an electric quality to it—that normally glowed like extra Christmas decorations among the deciduous trees and barren ground of the other houses in the neighborhood. But now, the ice covered his yard too, reducing it to the same dull glaze as its surroundings.

He wasn't home, but I had a key to his shed, and I knew he wouldn't mind if I borrowed his chainsaw. I left a note and carried the saw like a rifle over my shoulder as I started the trudge back home through the ice.

On the way I thought about the swing set we'd bought for Jannie not long after we'd moved into the neighborhood, how Cassie and I would take turns pushing her when she was small, and then how Jannie and her playmates would spend hours out there playing. Jannie lost interest in the swing set, of course, as she got older, but it sat there until her junior year of high school, until it was finally so rusty I dragged it to the street for the trash pickup.

When I got home I noticed that the pile of brush by the street had grown. The stuffed donkey was still there. I picked it up and carried it with me into the house.

"Where did all that brush come from?" I asked Cassie. I found her eating little squares of cheddar cheese and sipping white wine in front of a fire she'd built while I was gone.

"That man was back while you were out," she said between chews. "He hauled stuff out from the back. Not all of it, but some of the smaller limbs that didn't need to be cut."

"Did you ask him why he was doing it? Or who he was?"

"I was scared to go out there with him, though he looked nice." She took a sip of her wine. "Handsome, actually."

I held out the stuffed donkey. "Not as handsome as this little guy, I bet."

"How cute," she said, taking the donkey from me. "What's his name?"

"Eeyore," I said.

"Very original." She smiled and rubbed her hand over the donkey's head. "Where did you get him?"

Before I could answer we heard a bump on the side of the house. We listened for a moment and then heard footsteps on the roof.

I jerked open the front door and then walked carefully across the icy porch into the front yard, where I looked up at the roof. I could see a tree saw, a manual one, sliding back and forth across the limb that was draped over the wire. Beneath the saw, an arm in a blue jean jacket sleeve pumped up and down while the matching arm held the limb.

The rest of the person was on the other side of the roof peak, and I could just barely see the crown of a red wool cap and nothing else.

I called out, but I don't think he could hear me over the sound of the saw teeth scratching through the wood.

I went to the side of the house where I'd heard the bump, and I saw his ladder. Without really contemplating, I started up. I found myself standing beside him on the slope of the house in the back.

"Who are you?" I asked.

"Donnie Mattox," he said. "I just moved in down the street. I've been helping people out. You know, make a good first impression on the neighborhood and all that."

I wanted to ask if he hadn't thought about introducing himself first, but instead I asked, "Why us?"

"You look like you have more damage than most."

I think at this point I shifted my foot just a little to the right, but whatever caused it, I fell and slid on my stomach off the back of the roof and belly-flopped to the frozen, timber-covered ground of the back yard. It seemed to happen in slow motion, and I felt that unreal feeling you get when an emergency suddenly hits you blindside. For a moment it I seemed to be watching it happen on TV, to somebody else, but then the explosion of pain around my waist as I hit the ground snapped me back into the moment. I could hear Donnie asking over and over if I was all right, but I could only whimper. He soon appeared on the ground in front of where I lay; so did my wife. She bent down to me and put her hand on my forehead. The warmth felt good. I had regained my senses enough to say, "I'm okay, but I think I broke something." Donnie was calling an ambulance on his cell phone.

The fall must have somehow jarred my memory because I recalled that this was not the first time in my adult life I had been on a roof. The other time was when Cassie and I were dating. We must have been rising seniors in college, and I was visiting her at her parents' house during summer vacation. Her parents were out of town, and we had the ranch house with its pond and acreage to ourselves. The crickets and cicadas chimed loudly all around us in the warm air. Bullfrogs bellowed from the pond about fifty yards away. A whippoorwill begged in the distance. We shimmied up a tree that grew close to the house in the back. I had forgotten that I was actually agile once. We lay on the shingles, which were still warm from the daylight, and looked up at the stars. She wanted to make love right there, and I said it was too dangerous, that the slope was too steep, but she stripped off her t-shirt, and with a flash of her breasts she convinced me.

As Cassie looked at me now I could see her face was tight. She was fighting back tears. She took my right hand in both of hers. The warmth of her touch made me more aware of the cold and the pain in my side.

Days later I nursed a broken pelvis in bed, a kerosene heater on the floor beside me. I heard the refrigerator start up, and then I noticed that the hall light was on. The power was restored. The TV at the foot of the bed came on, and I saw Bob Barker talking into his microphone while a woman spun the big Price is Right wheel. School and business closings slid in a red band across the bottom of the TV screen. The ice was all melted, but the area was far from normal. Utility trucks from hundreds of miles away were working 'round the clock to restore power everywhere, but no one could say when everyone would have lights and heat.

Cassie brought in a tray of French toast and coffee. The coffee steamed from a chipped Disneyworld mug with "Dad" written in big letters. I remembered when Jannie bought that mug for me on our family trip to the Magic Kingdom. It was a small thing, this coffee mug, but with Jannie we'd quilted a life from small things. The French toast Cassie brought me now was also a small thing, but she could have brought me cereal and still felt as if she'd done her duty. I couldn't have blamed her if she had.

"I tried the insurance company again," she said. "Still busy."

I nodded. "We'll have to stay after them. They're not going to write checks to God-knows-how-many policyholders without a fight." She rubbed my forehead and gave me a smile that looked part genuine and part forced. Being allies against the insurance company was a start. It was good to feel on the same team with her again, no matter what the circumstance.

She had stayed by me in the hospital the whole time. Our conversations were somewhat labored, but we kept talking. And Jannie had called at least twice a day, putting us both in better spirits.

Over the TV now I heard the growl of a chainsaw somewhere close by. It was a sound that was becoming very familiar. Then the phone beside the bed rang. It was Jannie.

"Hey, old man. Ready to do some more sledless sledding on the roof?"

I smiled. "I retired. Going out with a bang."

"How do you feel today?"

"Thanks to Lortab and hot coffee, I'm feeling okay for the moment."

"We've had plenty of beer and sunshine down here in Orlando," she said. Their team had won, too.

"Too bad you have to head back north. It's still pretty cold up here."

"'Up here?' Dad, you're in South Carolina."

"Yeah, well, ice is ice."

"The Weather Channel says it's mostly melted."

"Yes." I heard the chainsaws working outside. "The ice is leaving. Just as soon as I heal, I'll start cleaning the yard." ✶

OLD COURT

➤ ELIZABETH COX

‒ ‒ ‒ ‒ ‒ ‒ ‒ ‒ ‒ ‒ ‒ ‒ ‒ ‒ ‒

The room, even at midday, held a romantic dimness as though it were always lit by a lantern. Sunlight hit the dark wood floor and mahogany table in a way that gave the room a yellow glow, and the optical illusion of a lantern was strong when the wind blew, changing the shadows so that light fought itself like boxers against the walls. But even with all the sunlight, there were corners that remained unlit.

Three chairs were arranged around a rug. The larger, more comfortable chair was my mother's; so was the table beside it—her favorite made of cherrywood. She kept her sewing on that table and would never let a glass or a bottle be set upon it. As I remember her table, and the yellow light of that room, it stands in my mind like a dream, becoming immemorial and ancient as a court.

The Civil War had been over for three years when my father died. I was nine, too young to be the man of the house. Sometimes my uncle would come. He would put his hand on my shoulder as if I were a grown man, and I liked for him to be there.

During our last summer and fall in that house, a shift of happenings began to occur. I was eleven then. Men came by on horseback. Strangers. They arrived in a flurry, as birds would, the horses jostling even as the men jumped from them. We never knew when to expect their arrival. This time, I could see from a low windowsill and count six of them at least, all going to the back of the house to dip one by one from the well. They could have just as easily robbed us. My mother's jewelry box didn't have much, but had a gold wedding band, and a watch with three diamond chips, and two pearl earrings given to her by an aunt who lived in New England.

There had been a light snow the night before, though it was October and unusual for cold weather to come that early in Mississippi. Marigolds still bloomed in the fields. The snow came around five in the morning but melted and was gone by ten.

"They've come back," I yelled toward the other room. My mother knew, her ears attuned to every danger. We lived in the house, alone, miles from town. All we had was the house, our garden out back, my mother's job at the piece-goods store, and small jobs I could take in summer months, a field lying fallow, and these men rushing to our well in bad times. The well had not filled up yet after the summer's drought. We had barely enough water for ourselves, and them taking all they could, then heading out—my mother relieved each time.

"We must go away soon," she would say, but found it hard to leave.

And when the men came, she hid herself where she could see the door but where she wouldn't be seen. She held a shotgun loaded and ready, pointed at the door. I often wondered if she would have turned herself loose to kill or maim, if she would actually pull back the trigger.

"They've come back," I yelled again, but I could see her already crouched between the large chair and table. Her hair was pulled up into a braid on the crown of her head, and she looked prettier than she had looked in months.

The men called obscenities back and forth, their talk like a thorn stuck in my mind. I hoped my mother wouldn't notice, thinking she must go out and grab them by their ears, swat each one for his remarks. In fact, I couldn't picture her failing to do this, so I wanted to warn them, lest she hear.

I knelt by the window, my eyes barely over the sill. I thought that only my eyes were over the sill, forgetting about the top of my head. The men walked around the yard in the openness of their desires. They wore boots in summer, and they wore boots now, only now they wore heavy coats and caps that fit tightly around their heads. The strong, flatland wind gave their clothes a heavy flutter, and the caps made their eyes seem wide, blank as owls.

Each man drank from a dipper beside the well, and I laughed because it was the dipper I let my dog drink from. I wondered where Buster was, since he usually barked and snapped at them. One man picked up a piece of leather. It was part of my father's belt that I had cut to make a collar for Buster. I hoped the man wouldn't take that last scrap, but as I saw him tuck it into the side pouch of his saddle I tried to forget about it. I didn't know how many times they might come back to the house, or what else they might do. We lived halfway between two towns, and even when my father was alive men would ride by and ask for water—but they always asked.

When one of the men saw me at the windowsill, he ran and hit the wood frame to scare me. My mother moved in the next room. I felt the sudden queasiness one feels just before throwing up, so I lay flat against the floorboards. Upon hearing them leave, I relaxed enough to count the cracks on the wall and thought about when Uncle Josh would come.

My uncle came out on Saturdays. He had never married, though I think he had women he lived with from time to time. He was tall, like my father, and had dark hair that never looked combed. My mother's hair was straight. At bedtime when she brushed it a hundred strokes, her voice grew musical. I think it was the only time she thought of herself as pretty. She threw her hair over her face and brushed it from the nape of her neck, then pushed it back. It was so long she could sit on it. And at those times, she talked and asked questions or listened to whatever I said without being busy, her expression as calm as soap.

My dad was a large man. I thought I would never be that large, and in fact I'm not. We would duck hunt all winter—my dad and me and Uncle Josh—and always on Christmas Eve. Christmas Eve morning, before the light, we would rise and eat the cold ham biscuits my mother left out. She said she was not getting up at any four o'clock in the morning just to fix breakfast. But she would prepare biscuits late at night and wrap them already piled with ham and butter, so that in the morning they were good, if not warm. And she always called from the bedroom anyway, at four-fifteen, "You boys need anything?" so that we could tell her the biscuits were fine, maybe the best she had ever made, because she had been up later than we had, fixing them. We thanked her in that way so she fell asleep satisfied.

Our duck pond was not really a pond, but a slough, a natural marshland forty yards wide and good for ducks. On almost any Saturday morning in the late fall, Uncle Josh came by with hip boots and gear, and we waded the fields the way we had done with my father, breaking the ice in places. Josh broke it as he stepped, without thinking. I broke it on purpose, going whichever way I saw unbroken patches so I could break them and hear them crack.

Sometimes Josh brought other men with him, but usually he took only me. He taught me the difference between a birch and a poplar, and would tell stories of my father, how they rode together in the war. He told how they named their horses after women they loved and that my dad named his horse Ruby after my mother, saying if he was going into something he might not come back from he would go into it with Ruby. Each time Josh told me this he said it with such fervor that I wondered if that time of his life was the best and did he long for it. Once I asked him, and he stared at me for a moment as though I had shown him a truth he hadn't expected.

"Maybe," he said. He pulled me to stand close to him. "But I don't wish for it." Our hip boots touched. It was awkward to stand that close, because of our boots, but I stood, not moving. I even put my arm around his waist, not out of love but to keep from falling. He said, "I only meant to give you an idea of it, and how we were afraid."

"You never said about that."

"I didn't?"

"No."

"It was when you saw them coming," he began, and I settled in to listen. "Saw them coming toward you with what you had, maybe more, and bent on doing to you what you would do to them." His eyes went back to remember. "It killed something in me, and in your father, too, I think. Though not as much." He looked as though he were telling something different now. "I mean," he said, "the things we had to do."

I didn't know what he meant. "Those men came back," I told him.

"They kicked Buster and hurt his ribs." Josh didn't say anything, and I wondered if he knew where he was and if we would hunt anymore that day.

We did. We hunted three more hours. The sun came all the way up but couldn't warm us because our boots and jackets were wet. Our bodies were dry, though, and warm enough, if not as warm as they would be. We walked back with greenheads hanging from the back satchels of our vests, and talked about how the house would smell like mincemeat and how the heat would hold our faces the same as the cold did, only better.

The table was set, the floor swept and slightly damp from being mopped. My mother met us at the door to prevent us from dragging in our boots. We left boots, shirts, and pants on the steps, and she made us wash up. It always struck me as strange that we had to be clean for meals, but it didn't matter much if we were dressed. My mother wore a skirt and flowered blouse. We wore long underwear, though Josh put on pants. If company came, I put on pants too.

"Your father is dead," my mother told me one day when I got in from school. She sat in a chair where she always sat, so that when I walked in from school she was what I saw first. I saw her that day, too, but she had her arms outstretched before her, leaning toward me, and I went into them as deep as I could. Then she pushed back, and I saw in her face the very root of her disbelief.

"How?" I finally asked, but she had already begun to tell me.

"He lifted lumber onto the wagon. A heavy load, most likely." She sounded admonitory, if not critical. "And it fell back on him," she said. "He climbed onto the wagon, and logs rolled across him. When they lifted the load off his chest, he was already gone." She began to cry softly. I wanted to but couldn't. Instead, I watched tears squeeze out from those tight-closed eyelids, falling quick and soft between us. She kept her arms around me, not even attempting to cover her face as I would have done. It was as though she could not be embarrassed or ashamed, only sad. She grieved for my dad better than I did, for I refused to bear it for almost a year. And finally, when I could talk of him and show tears, my mother's tears were gone.

The men on horseback came during the summer months and on that one October day, but it was Christmas Eve when they came by at night. My mother and I attended the Christmas pageant in town and got home late, ten o'clock. The men probably had been there already and found the house empty, not wanting anything there but wanting something to do with us, a mischief.

My mother would stay up late and put out whatever I received for Christmas, pretending still that it was brought in secret, both of us pretending, because there could be only one or two gifts, and the surprise was all. So we held to this, partly because she wanted to and never mentioned doing differently, and partly because I wanted to prolong the belief. Besides, most of the time my mother thought of me as a child. It was only now and then that she stood back, even stepped back physically from me, and said, "You look like your father when you do that," and she looked a little longer, not seeing him exactly, but seeing me in a different way. I always liked those times, because she wouldn't hug me to her as though she needed something I couldn't give anymore, but instead would ask me to perform some task that she said had become too difficult for her.

We were not home fifteen minutes before we heard them, the hooves and galloping we had heard before but always in the daytime. I had put on my pajamas, soft, heavy material that kept me warmer sometimes than my clothes. My mother still had not undressed, but she had set the table for the next morning's breakfast. I hoped she might brush her hair.

When I entered the kitchen, she put out the lamp. For a moment, neither of us could see, and she reached through the dark for me, whispering, "Luther, Luther."

"I'm here." But her hands had already found me.

"Get the shotgun." She went in another direction as I fingered my way toward the mantel and above it to where the shotgun hung. It was always loaded.

She came toward me again, both of us now able to see each other's shadows. The moon was full, and the room flooded with its light. The floor shone white as water, and I almost expected, when I stepped, to hear the crack of ice.

I handed the shotgun to her. She took it with one hand, her arm seeming longer in the moonlight, thinner than it really was. With her other hand, she pushed something toward me.

"Merry Christmas," she said.

I could not see it but knew it was a rifle, and wondered how she would pay for it. A Winchester 66. It was what I wanted but hadn't imagined getting. I stroked the wooden stock and the silky black barrel and felt sorry about the present I had for her. It wasn't enough.

The men had stopped their horses. They didn't go around to the well, nor did they come with the flurry of their usual visits.

"Is it loaded?" I asked.

She said it was.

I readied myself in a position below the sill, and wondered if I would have to kill a man and if it would kill something in me. I didn't feel the hate I thought I would need to feel. The door was being tried—no knock, just breaking in—and I felt a rising nausea.

I squeezed the trigger, not at the door but out the window. The breaking of glass was all I heard. I squeezed again and again and the shots came out like tears from those tight-closed eyelids. My mother called my name and at last, after what seemed an interminable wait, the noise leveled out against the night's quiet. But before full silence fell again, I could see in that holy Christmas light a horse rising up, then dropping, his legs crumpling as paper would, paper legs to hold his heavy body and head. And I heard his sound, after the sound the gun made, a whinnying too high-pitched for anything but pain. A pure calling for help, and his knees bending to that call.

"Damn." One man ran to the horse. "Damn." He looked down at it, a dark heap like coal. My mother came to the window. The man at the door yelled to his friend, and they both climbed onto the other horse. We watched as they rode off.

"They are drunk," my mother said. Her first words. But she was quiet about what I had done. And finally, when she lit the lamp, minutes after the men had galloped off, her face was like chalk. And she tried to praise me, as though what I had done was well thought out and what I had planned to do.

But it wasn't. It was what I did. And she thought I had decided to shoot but not to shoot at the man. She thought my mind had made the decision not to kill him.

"You decided," she said, giving me credit. "You made that decision from some old court in your mind. I am proud."

"But, Mama—"

"I am proud." She would always see me better than I was.

The next morning when I went out I knew I had to dig a hole big enough to bury the horse where he lay. He could never be moved, not by me nor my mother, so I dug most of the day, and later in the evening my mother helped. It took two days to dig a hole big enough to shove him into. By then the flies had some, and the sun had begun to bake his skin.

My mother and I wore kerchiefs on our faces to keep from breathing the odor. We were glad the air was cold and kept the flesh from rotting too quickly. I had uncinched the saddle and was able to pull it from under the horse, but I couldn't loosen the bit from his mouth. His teeth had locked shut around it. Then I remembered my father opening a horse's mouth once by squeezing the sides where the mouth began, and when I did that, the bit fell out. We threw the bridle and saddle into the hole with him, and the halter strap, but I kept the blanket that had covered his back and protected him from sores.

The day we pushed him into the hole, it was raining. My mother packed our trunk and filled the wagon with all she could. Josh and the man from the piece-goods store came to help us bring our furniture to the new house.

We did not move far, but into town where there were lawns and neighbors. A few weeks went by before I remembered that I had failed to give my mother her gift. We rode back to the house, which no one lived in now but had been sold with the land. The mound of dirt rose fresh, and we shuddered to think what was beneath it. The door of the house had blown open, and snow or rain had ruined the front entrance. The romantic dimness had gone.

I climbed to pull a loose brick from the fireplace and removed a small, rectangular box wrapped in paper with shiny red flowers. My mother loved the paper and praised it. I wanted and took the praise.

The box held a necklace, its pendant the shape of a leaf. It was yellow gold and opened like a locket. When she opened it, there was a picture inside, the only one I could find, which was of herself when she was ten years old.

She sat down on an old crate, and I stood close beside her. "Put it on me," she said. So I did. She pressed it flat against her chest. Then she turned her head toward the window and fingered the leaf, opening and closing it to hear the soft click. But when she turned her gaze back to me, her eyes were so full of admiration that I felt like a small god. She put her hand on my back, and the smile that came to her face was like a crescent, each corner turning upward as if it had been drawn there.

I smiled too but tried to pretend I had smiled at something else— outside maybe—a bush. Then I looked to see the pane still broken, the simply rounded mount of dirt, the dark heap beneath it that would stay beneath me, like something I would have to stand on. But all around us the rest of the land lay flat, and as far as I could see, it went out straight before us. *

ALSO EXPERT TOUR GUIDE

> THOMAS PIERCE

When Elsa Cunningham—owner of the state's most successful chain of funeral homes—said she was going to be our state's next senator, I believed her. Before you laugh, let me explain: I was barely out of college at the time. And what Cunningham needed most was a win here in Spoke County, so as a native son I felt ideally situated to help.

Yes, I was aware Spoke County had voted Republican for almost fifty years. But that didn't bother me—mainly because it didn't bother Tara.

For six months Tara basically ran Elsa's operation in Spoke—the phone banks and fundraisers, neighborhood meetings, volunteer workshops, pancake suppers, cocktail parties. Tara gave me an office next to hers. Together, we posted signs in yards that hadn't even asked for them. We knocked on doors in white and black neighborhoods. We drove to the outskirts of town where people are just as likely to aim a shotgun at your heart as they are to jot their name on a clipboard.

Once, they sent Tara and me down to Columbia to pick up boxes of leaflets with instructions not to bring them back to the office. Instead, we were directed to leave our boss's car behind a bar downtown with the keys on the tire. Naturally, we peeked in the boxes on the way back, and sure enough, these were the infamous *Did You Know Russell King has TWO Families?* leaflets—two pictures of our opponent, posed with a different family in each. If you don't believe me, I swiped a leaflet and still have it somewhere, I think. I suppose I do feel a little guilty knowing we helped orchestrate one of the dirtiest campaign tricks in our state's history, but politics is politics.

Besides, Elsa Cunningham lost the election.

First, the office phones were disconnected. Next they asked us to forfeit our Blackberries and laptops. We dumped all the extra yard signs into recycling bins. Elsa sent us all away with short, friendly notes, and two days after losing, I'm told she retired to her family's second home on the coast to recuperate.

I opened her letter in the privacy of my apartment, sulking in my boxer shorts, cereal milk dripping down onto my open de Tocqueville. I managed to get through one paragraph before lighting it on fire and dropping the flaming paper in the toilet.

Look: in the aftermath of the election, I perfected the art of self-pity. I had a blog that none of my friends knew about and wrote long, spiraling treatises on the failures of democracy and all that. I smoked Parliaments on the roof and ate Chinese food twice a day. And I probably would have blown through all my campaign checks that way if Tara hadn't come over and told me we were going on a trip.

"My brother thinks I should come home now, Carp, and I'm not ready for that yet," she explained.

"So where do you propose we go?"

"I've got this uncle," she said. "Lives down in the Everglades."

Tara wasn't from Spoke, and this wasn't her first campaign. She'd done this all before, but I don't think that dulled the sting of defeat. Over the course of the campaign, she'd basically stayed over at my apartment every night, but trust me, nothing ever happened. She'd change into her tiny green gym shorts, climb into bed, and curl up against me like some aloof house cat. Her long blonde hair would tickle my back when she flipped, and even Nyquil couldn't put me to sleep at night.

Those sleepovers were the best kind of torture—filled with a miserable longing that I suspect never really dies but just migrates to some other part of the body to hibernate. I'm pretty sure my nights with Tara moved into my lower intestines and even now, years later, I still worry that if I stretch the wrong way after a long run, all those old feelings might come rushing back up my bloodstream to drown my heart.

Tara had been engaged—years before—to a FedEx driver who'd died in some kind of car crash. I never got all the details. She had a tattoo of a piano keyboard on her left shoulder blade, and on Sundays she would spend the entire day methodically working through the paper, article by article. She preferred taxis home after dark, spoke a little Russian, and one time confessed a love of snakes, especially the ones that swim. Her curly blonde hair would come out of its ponytail on the weekend, but in the office she dressed modestly, pant suits and shirts with wide, white collars. And she was older, of course. The campaign threw her a birthday party with cakes, hats, and booze when she turned thirty-two.

People whispered about our arrangement. A volunteer once referred to Tara as my girlfriend. That night, she didn't stay over.

"My place is just so empty," she explained at my door the next night for the one-hundredth time, handbag over her shoulder. "But Carp, you don't want me like that, trust me."

Ours was a balancing act. She'd tell me how it was, and I'd just nod my head for fear of scaring her away. If the most I could hope for were sleepless nights and conversations over waffles, then I'd take them and not complain.

So that's where we still stood when—desperate to shake our post-election misery and shared fear of the future—we launched our trip to the Everglades.

"His name is Brick," she told me outside of Savannah.

"Uncle Brick."

"That's right, and he knows alligators better than anybody."

"Right."

"He does, Carp. I've been meaning to get down there ever since I graduated. He says he'll take me out in a canoe, and we'll see plenty of them."

"Is Brick a nickname?"

"Don't know. It's been Brick as long as I can think back. Brace yourself, he's a strange guy. Mom says he lived in Seattle for about a decade but never talks about it anymore. He also used to race speedboats—the really fast kind that flip all the time, but he never flipped, I don't think. These days he mostly moves up and down the coast. Last summer Mom said he was down in Key West painting houses."

I began ticking off a mental checklist of everything we might need out there on the water for survival if Brick got us lost. I think Tara sensed the sudden outbreak of doubt in the way I planted my feet on the floorboard, like this was a driver's-school car and I had a brake of my own.

"Don't worry," she said, "he's also an expert tour guide."

Most of Tara's extended family lived in Florida. She'd gone to college there and then moved to Missouri for a congressional race, then to Kansas for another. She was a campaign veteran, though none of her candidates had ever actually won.

"I remember this family reunion like ten years ago," she said. "A gator got stuck up under the house, so Brick crawled under, dragged it out, and tied a garden hose around its mouth. My cousins loved it. Uncle Brick was kind of our hero."

"What's the difference between an alligator and a crocodile?"

"That's a question you'll have to ask Brick."

Around Orlando, we refueled Tara's Honda Civic and swapped seats. I was behind the wheel when we reached Everglades City that night.

"Uncle Brick told Mom there's an RV park with tent sites across the street from the Ranger's station. We can get a site there and then go pick him up in the morning. He doesn't live in town exactly."

A convenience store doubled as the campground office, but it was closed. We found an empty lot next to the road and pitched our tent. Across the street, a neon sign above a liquor store flashed *Budweiser*, on and off, and the red and blue flittered eerily through the rain fly once we were inside our sleeping bags and ready for bed.

"You sleepy?" she asked.

"Not at all."

"Think that liquor store's open?"

The liquor store was open, and I bought us a bottle of gin and some paper cups. I met Tara at the nearest picnic table and poured a dozen or so generous shots, gin drops sprinkling all over the wood and our legs. One by one, we knocked them back. Tara looked happier than she had in months. We talked about alligators and peat fires, and we didn't dare utter the name Elsa Cunningham. That name was off-limits. I felt human again. Another shot. The humidity made Tara's hair curlier than usual around her small, flushed face. I could hardly look at her without smiling a little.

The neon sign flashed on and off, on and off, and my head spun with the sound of mosquitoes in my ear. Another shot.

Then she said, *time for bed*, and took me by the hand to the tent. We left the gin bottle open on the table.

I won't lie: I don't remember all the details of what happened next. But what I do remember is a whole lot of zipping: tent doors and windows, sleeping bags and blue jeans, all that zipping whirling in my ears, a chorus of metal teeth. We yanked our bags close together, sliding back and forth across the slick nylon floor as we messed with straps and buttons, and I ran my hand through her curls and over her back and down her cheeks, and we shoved out of our underwear, and when I woke up in the morning, I was naked, halfway out my sleeping bag, and alone.

The door flapped in the breeze. I counted at least seven mosquito bites along my arm. I struggled into my clothes and stretched outside the tent.

Tara returned with a grocery bag—a loaf of French bread, Nutella, and a quart of milk.

"Ready for some wildlife?"

"Sure," I said.

"Good, 'cause it's time for you to meet Uncle Brick."

She had his address on a scrap of paper, and we followed the directions out of town—down a dirty highway.

Neither of us dared mention what had transpired in the tent.

She'd bought Advil and water, too, so I washed a couple of pills down with a giant swig.

According to Tara's mom, Brick was living with a woman named Glenn, which first reminded me of the astronaut-senator, John Glenn. But when Brick's Glenn opened the door in white sweatpants and a bathing suit top barely tied around her neck, I couldn't really imagine her on a spacewalk. She had an iPod wrapped around her upper arm like a nicotine patch. Her house was small but isolated from all the other nearby homes by a thick growth of bushes, pine trees, and vines. A television set roared in a back room. The doormat said, *Whatchu Want Sucka?* I'm not joking.

"I suppose you're looking for Brick?" she said, taking her headphones out.

Tara nodded. So did I.

"Well, he's not here. Hasn't been for about a week actually."

Glenn stepped all the way out of the house, joining us on the stoop, where an electric bug zapper dangled from the awning next to an empty hummingbird feeder.

"Any idea where we can find him?" Tara asked.

"How should I know? He comes and goes. Hey, you want something to eat? I've got eggs in the pot."

"That's alright," we said.

Glenn flipped her blonde hair over the top of her head, leaning forward to retie the bathing suit strap around her freckled neck in a fancier loop. A cloud shifted above, the sun shone brighter, and I could see Glenn's hair was more white than blonde.

"Look," she said, "his canoe's behind the house. You can take it if you want."

Tara and I exchanged looks. I could tell she was disappointed. Maybe she felt like she owed me something and without our intrepid Everglades guide this whole trip might not amount to much—unless you counted the night before, but I don't think Tara was counting.

The canoe had been covered with a green tarp but a number of holes had allowed rainwater to flood the hull. We tipped it over, a soupy mess of algae and mosquito larvae and water and pine straw gushing over the sides to soak into the grass. The smell was awful—like old bananas, boiled meat, and sweat. Glenn watched us empty the contents and drag the boat toward the car. Once we got it there, neither of us knew what to do with it.

"I've got some bungees," Glenn said and went back into the house.

On the count of three, we hoisted the aluminum boat up in the air above our heads and placed it on the top of Tara's Civic, open-side down. The metals scratched, and I thought my head might collapse from the sound.

Glenn came back with the cords and helped us cocoon the canoe with bungees, cords running over the hull and through the cracked windows. I remembered some twine in the trunk and used that to tie the bow to the grill of the car so it wouldn't slip off the back when we accelerated.

"Paddles are up against the house," Glenn said.

I grabbed those and forced them diagonally in the backseat over Tara's stuff, white oars hanging out the open window.

"Would you tell my uncle that we're staying at the campground near the liquor store?" Tara asked. "In case he shows up?"

"Tell him if I see him."

"Thanks for letting us use the canoe," I called as we climbed back into the car.

"Don't get lost out there. Ten thousand islands, you know?"

"We'll be alright," I said, car tires crunching over the gravel drive.

The only radio station I could pick up on the way back to town carried pop country, so we listened to that. We didn't say much until we were almost back to the liquor store.

"I'm sorry about my uncle. He's never exactly been the most reliable guy, but Mom promised me he'd be there, so I'm sorry."

"I don't mind. We got the boat at least, right?"

The tent was still pitched on site number four, and the gin bottle glimmered in the sun on the picnic table where we'd left it. I screwed the top back on and stuffed it under the passenger seat for later. Across the road we could see the Everglades Ranger station and behind that was a put-in for smaller boats. We scouted it out, then slid the canoe off the car and dropped it by the tent.

Tara said she wanted to wait one more day, just in case Brick decided to show. So we walked down the street to a bait and grocery store with a sign for hot fish sandwiches that we'd spotted on the way back from Glenn's. We grabbed a table, ordered beer and sandwiches with hot sauce.

"When did you know Elsa was going to lose?" I asked her.

"When they asked me to come down," she said and laughed.

"No, really."

"Probably the night we went to Columbia," she said. "Those leaflets. That was the end."

After lunch we napped in the tent but stayed on our respective sleeping bags. I rolled over once, breathed heavy on her arm, but she didn't move. I couldn't tell if she was playing opossum.

We woke up near dark, both feeling groggy. I turned on the car for a minute to check the time and feel the air conditioning on my cheeks. We ambled back to the same grocery for another round of fish sandwiches. One of the local guys—dirty khakis and a short beard—eyed Tara the whole meal. And when I went to pay the bill, he offered to buy her a beer. I swear she almost took him up on it before joining me at the register.

"You could have, you know. I don't care."

Both of us knew that was a lie, and she didn't answer.

Back at the campsite, she said she wanted to read for a while and crawled inside the tent with a flashlight and magazines. I smoked a cigarette on the picnic table and sipped on the gin.

"Sure you don't want some?" I called.

"No, thanks," she said from inside the tent. "I'm still feeling last night."

Eventually I joined her and kept my eyes open as long as I could, but when I dozed off, she was still reading her magazines.

The next morning, I woke up first, feeling brave. I watched her breathe and even stroked her arm a little. She finally squinted her eyes open, clasped my hand, smiled, but then let it go.

"Listen—"

"Let's take the boat out," I said.

"I don't even know where to take it."

"We'll figure it out."

Tara was hopeful Brick might still show up and convinced me to wait for a few more hours. But by noon, after we'd shared yet another round of sandwiches, I started dragging the canoe across the street on my own, metal attacking the pavement. I was aiming for the Ranger's station and the put-in.

"Okay, okay," she relented, picking up the other end. "But we're not going out far."

I stepped into the brackish water first and let my feet sink a little in the muck, squishiness between my toes. Probably wasn't more than a foot deep but I couldn't see a thing beneath my ankles. We guided the canoe over the gravel and down into the water.

She steadied the boat as I hopped in the front with both paddles and a water bottle. Tara shoved us off and jumped into the back, rocking the boat hard to the left. I laughed but only a little because I really did think we were going in.

The boat still smelled funny—like we'd dug it up out of a grave.

We stuck close to the shore at first, messing with our paddles in the water and finding our rhythm. She steered us in zigzags for the first mile but had the hang of it by the time we had paddled to the end of the Chokoloskee peninsula and reached more open water. The bay stretched in all directions. Far across the dark water, we could see another shore and to our left were small mangrove islands. Herons stepped through the tall grass, and some birds I didn't recognize rested on buoys bobbing in the wake. I wished for some binoculars and a nature book—or an Uncle Brick.

"We have to go back between the islands to find any gators," she said.

We aimed for the mangrove. Our paddles sliced through the water and for a while, the island didn't seem to curve at all. I felt like we were moving in a straight line until I looked across the bay at the other shore and realized we were slowly turning. My bearing was all skewed. We followed the curve of one island before turning between two more, deeper and deeper into the maze of tributaries and mangrove. We floated into a tinier cove where the branches on either side of us reached out to scrape our boat and shoulders like long, curly fingernails.

"You know where we're going?" I asked.

"Kind of," she said. "Watch for movement up ahead. Sometimes they'll dive off the banks when they hear us coming."

I waited and waited, almost breathless, but saw no flicker of activity up ahead, no disturbance of the water save the tiny spiders that skittered across the surface. Leaves and sticks collected in dark crevices of the mangrove root along the shore, and the sun was broken by the lattice-work growth overhead, creating a grid of orange and yellow on the green water. I honestly felt like we'd stepped back in time to the Triassic—like we weren't looking for gators but some kind of elusive dinosaur-bird.

We were totally alone out there.

I had the urge to stand up, but by then branches hung so low that we seemed to be traveling through a swampy tunnel. With the vines and trees closing in on us, I suffered a momentary bout of what I can only describe as an overload of smallness—a feeling that the tributary was just some coffee spill dribbling down a kitchen cabinet somewhere and we were a speck of coffee grind traveling with it. You know how it is: like the universe and everything in it but you is expanding simultaneously in a big way—you just keep getting smaller and smaller, losing control all the while, and that's when I almost rocked the boat over.

"Watch it," she said, but by then we'd already regained our balance. "Listen, maybe it's time to head back now. It's going to be dark soon, I think."

"But we haven't seen any gators yet."

Look: up to that point, I could have cared less about seeing an alligator. And honestly, I was ready to head back, too. I don't know why, but what I suddenly desired more than anything was to see a gator up close. If we could, I intended to steer up beside one, learn how it sneaks through the water, and pat its belly like a stray dog.

"We might see one on the way back," she said. "You never know."

She turned the boat sharply, and we had to grab the branches above to spin ourselves in the opposite direction—that's how narrow this tributary was. Tara started moving us forward but I grabbed a tree limb again and stopped us dead in the water. Her paddle fought to move us forward.

"Carp, stop. What are you doing?"

"Just messing around, sorry," I said, and let us go.

The sun dipped behind the tallest trees.

Maybe what happened next could have been avoided with a map—or maybe not. All those mangrove islands are identical. Folks get turned around out there all the time. Plus, I hadn't paid much attention on the way out. When Tara started paddling faster and talking less, I knew we were lost.

One funny thing about moving in the near-darkness is how your senses sharpen. All the sounds—the mosquitoes in my ears and our paddles splashing in the water—were amplified. I caught a salty whiff of ocean breeze that moved through the islands like a supper smell. And in the eventual darkness, all the distant, amorphous shapes became alligators in my head. The stars above were ballot boxes, ready to be checked. When the boat floated over a loose log bobbing in the water, banging along the bottom of the boat, Tara yelped a little. I did, too. I turned to watch it pop back up behind us in the water, but it didn't. To this day, I wonder if we struck a sleeping alligator, if that's even possible.

No matter how desperately we hammered at the water, our boat seemed to stall. I charted our painfully slow progress against the shore. Years later I read about the power of the tide down there, how you're supposed to schedule your outings based on a table, and looking back on it, I'm pretty sure we were fighting a deep and sinister tide that night.

"About the other night," I said, without realizing I was going to say it. "We don't have to talk about it ever. I'm okay with that, you know?"

"Aren't we kind of talking about it now?"

"Suppose we are, yeah. It's just that I—"

"Can we talk about this once we're back on land? I mean, is this really the time?"

"Probably not the time," I admitted.

I paddled harder, trying to match her strokes. Behind me, muffled by the wind and water against the aluminum hull, I could hear her crying. Hell, she may have been praying. Call me mean-spirited, call me callous, but I didn't turn around to assure her we'd be alright. Even then, I suspected Tara wasn't going to stay in Spoke—that she'd find some other campaign and that my days as an operative were over.

Look: we had this rule back when we'd go out canvassing door-to-door, which was kind of a joke around the office but was also good advice. After you knock on a door, you stay quiet, ear trained for one of two sounds: a shotgun being cocked or a dog growling with a certain kind of snarl—a low bark that you can just tell is dripping with saliva. If that's what you hear, don't wait for the door to crack, just run back to the car and go. Drop whatever signs or letters or leaflets you've got stuffed under your arm and go. Never worth losing blood for a vote that's not going to put you over the top, we'd say, and I'm ashamed to admit it, but if I learned anything worth knowing at all from Elsa Cunningham's failed bid for senate, it might be that.

So sitting in the boat that night, Tara went on crying uninterrupted.

Water trickling down the paddle and soaking my arms and legs, a pool of water collecting around my naked feet, I didn't realize then that if I wanted any kind of resolution, this would be my only chance. I couldn't foresee how the next morning I'd wake up in the tent with a strange impulse to hitch a ride to the Greyhound station and buy a forty-seven-dollar ticket back to Spoke—without leaving so much as a note to explain myself. And I couldn't predict how crossing the Georgia state line in that bus, I'd begin to doubt my decision, and how months after that, I would determine not to call because surely she'd heard me as I packed my bag that morning, zipping and rustling beside her in the tent. Surely she'd been pretending all along—I'd later convince myself— to be asleep.

During that last hour of quiet paddling in the dark, I suppose there's no way I could have anticipated any of the agony and regret to come. When we did emerge at last from the mangrove, we could see the distant but beautiful lights of the Chokoloskee peninsula, milky along the horizon. But I knew nobody—not Uncle Brick, Elsa Cunningham, or anybody else—would be waiting to help drag the boat up on shore and tell us, yes, at least this part of the trip was over and done with. No one would be waiting to tell us where not to go from here. ✳

A TOUCH OF BLUE

> NORMAN POWERS

Lucille is sitting in her apartment this morning, watching reruns on television and thinking about time. She is thinking that time has a certain rhythm, like a symphony—no, like several symphonies, all played end-to-end; and she is thinking how you start out in life believing you're the conductor, setting the arrangement and tempo, and how the moment comes when you realize the orchestra's not paying attention anymore; that you've moved away from the podium and that you're sitting in the audience watching someone else up there, while you've become helpless, no longer in control.

It seems peculiar to Lucille that this train of thought should have been stimulated by an episode of "Andy Griffith." It's the one in which Andy is forced to eat three separate spaghetti dinners at three separate houses, all because he's too polite to refuse invitations from three separate people for the same evening. He's on his third dinner now, and looking clearly distressed—even trying to give Opie some of the spaghetti from his plate. Andy is obviously not in control in this episode, and Lucille feels strangely sympathetic. She is sure this is one of the later episodes, which just proves her point about the passing of time.

Today is the third Tuesday of the month, which is the day Lucille's children have designated as Hairdresser Day. Melinda makes the appointment for her each month, always at eleven o'clock, and makes sure to call the day before to remind her. "Remember what tomorrow is?" Melinda always says, and, "Tell her not to use so much rinse this time."

Lucille has to admit that she has been waiting for this third Tuesday of the month for three weeks, and that she has been sitting here waiting for eleven o'clock since seven-thirty. This is the rhythm that controls her life now, measured out in hairdresser appointments and *TV Guide* listings. Before, when Henry was alive, her life was different. Then, she stood squarely at the podium, baton in hand, coordinating dinner parties, family crises, anniversaries, funerals, trips abroad. "Check with the social secretary," Henry would tell people, grinning. "We'll have to ask the headmistress," the children would say to their friends. Now, the children say, "Take it easy, Mother," and "We'll take care of everything, Ma." The children chose this apartment for her, sold the house, and installed her here with the others, all watching time slow down.

Robert always wants to pick her up on Hairdresser Day and drive her the three blocks to The Beauty Spot Spa and Salon, but Lucille has so far succeeded in discouraging him. Robert's been fired from his job, and Lucille thinks he should be out looking for another one instead of ferrying her around town. Besides, that disagreeable girlfriend is always with him, the one with the stringy hair and the funny name. Felicity? Freya? Anyway, some sort of odd "F" name. Robert has inherited nothing of his father's eye for women, Lucille thinks, and she can admit to herself now that some of Henry's mistresses were really quite beautiful. He was always discreet, and it was only by accident that Lucille saw one or two of them.

But Robert ... Lucille remembers the procession of anemic, whispering girls at Robert's side, all of whom could have used a dash of make-up and a few years at a decent finishing school, girls who were secretaries and manicurists, and a few who might have been something quite different, although Lucille doubts Robert would ever have the money for that sort of thing. Robert has made it plain that his *amours* are none of his mother's business. Lucille is grateful for this, and for the fact that she has so far avoided riding in the same car with Miss F.

Lucille has now moved from the living room to the dressing table in her bedroom—the dressing table Henry bought for her in that little shop in Paris—and has begun fixing herself up. Melinda has tried on several occasions to confiscate her jars and tubes and atomizers.

"Honestly, Mother, at *your* age!" Melinda always says.

"*Especially* at my age," Lucille always says back; but she refrains from pointing out that Melinda—never a pretty child—should do *something* with her pasty skin and thin lips and eyebrows that look like pencil smudges. Melinda has the worst features of both her parents, sad to say, and Lucille is frankly not surprised her daughter has never attracted a suitable young man.

In another moment of powerlessness, Lucille once allowed herself to be taken to one of Melinda's feminist meetings, and they'd had to stand up in front of everyone while Melinda spouted some sort of nonsense about mother-daughter bonding. Lucille remembers nothing of the kind—not in the recent past, certainly, and not when Melinda was a child. She remembers scenes during visits to Melinda's boarding school, and the two and a half weeks Melinda disappeared in Europe— the German police were *so* cooperative—and Melinda's affair with The Crook. "Damian wasn't a criminal, Mother," Melinda points out, whenever Lucille mentions him. "He was a political activist, that's all." The Crook had dumped Melinda after two months and disappeared to God knows where—probably to one of those South American countries where there's always so much trouble.

Lucille is dressed by ten-thirty and on her way to the elevator when she meets Mrs. Simmons, who, for reasons beyond Lucille's comprehension, seems to be continually shuffling between her apartment down the hall and the incinerator room at the end of the corridor. She does this so many times a day, week after week, month after month, that Lucille is convinced nothing can be left in her apartment except a few sticks of furniture and the pink housecoat Mrs. Simmons always wears.

"Off to the hairdresser, dear?" Mrs. Simmons says. "I can always tell, you know. By your clothes."

Lucille suddenly realizes this is quite true. Unconsciously, she always wears the blue pleated skirt and chiffon blouse on Hairdresser Day, along with the alligator bag and black pumps. She watches Mrs. Simmons disappear down the hallway toward the incinerator with her rattling, mysterious brown paper parcel, her housecoat ruffling around her thin, white legs.

Lucille goes back to the apartment and changes into the red two-piece, with a white bag and matching shoes. She knows the hairdresser will report this minor breach of routine.

"She didn't use too much rinse, did she?" Melinda wants to know. The phone had rung just moments after Lucille got home, since Melinda knows to the minute the schedule she's created for her mother, just as Lucille knows the amount of rinse used is not the real reason for the call. But she says sweetly, "Oh, no. It looks just fine." She waits.

"Delores says you looked different today," Melinda finally says, tentatively.

"Oh? Did you talk to her?" Melinda's impatience with the game is already wearing thin, but Lucille keeps the smile from her voice, and says, "Different? How different?"

"Of course I talked to her. You know I always check and make sure you got there and left safely," Melinda says. "Anyway, she says she'd never seen the clothes you were wearing." Melinda speaks as if Lucille had arrived at the Beauty Spot dressed in chain mail, and Lucille is pleased.

"Well, I hope I'm still capable of choosing my own wardrobe, dear," Lucille says, with just the right amount of exasperation. "I mean, it's not like I walked in there wearing those ripped jeans of yours with my knees sticking out. Anyone would think you couldn't afford decent clothes." The line is silent while Melinda considers the implications of this little rebellion, so Lucille, with another tingle of excitement, presses on. "And don't tell me those horrid things are what everyone wears, dear. You're not everyone, are you?" She considers bringing up The Crook again, but Melinda is somehow following her logic and says, hurriedly, "I'll talk to you later," and hangs up.

She had seen the Paris dressing table during one of her frequent rambles around the Marais, leisurely strolls when Henry had to commandeer the hotel room for business meetings. Henry always gave her money for these little expeditions which Lucille, by their seventh or eighth visit to Paris, came to regard as a sort of bribe. She had hated herself at first for thinking that way, but that was before she'd returned earlier than usual, only a few minutes early, but in time to see the waiting limousine in front of the hotel, Henry sweeping down the steps toward it, one hand casually slung around the waist of the Blue Lady. Lucille doesn't recall, after all these years, if the Blue Lady was actually wearing that particular color. The name had nothing to do with her clothes, anyway, but with the drooping shoulders, the sad, vacant eyes and expressionless mouth. Even after all these years, Lucille wonders what great tragedy could have so borne down on those white, frail shoulders. She had allowed herself just the hint of a smile when Henry kissed her lightly, and Lucille remembers being, to her surprise, proud of Henry, *her* Henry, lifting such gloom for even a moment.

She had waited until Henry went back inside, then caught up with him in the lobby. "Was it an enjoyable meeting?" she had asked him, not innocently at all, but with the slightest of pauses, just the hint of an emphasis on the word "meeting." She remembered watching his eyes flick toward the door, the little patch of red that rose on each cheek. Then she told him about the table, how she hadn't had enough money to buy it, how she'd pleaded with the shopkeeper to hold it until tomorrow.

"Tomorrow?" Henry had said. "Why wait until tomorrow?" and he had taken her arm and led her gently back toward the door.

The morning after Hairdresser Day, Lucille meets Mrs. Simmons again in the hallway on her daily shuffle to the incinerator room, and Lucille feels compelled to ask what she is carrying in the brown sack.

"Yesterday's newspaper," Mrs. Simmons says, without surprise or hesitation. "One of the *TV Guides* I always have next to the bed," she continues, "in case I can't sleep. The shell bits from my boiled egg. I *always* start the day with a boiled egg." She stops and thinks for a moment, apparently afraid she might leave something out. "I think that's all. This recycling business is a lot of nonsense, if you ask me. Better to just be careful what you throw away." She peers at Lucille, her brown eyes ballooning behind the thick lenses of her glasses. "I never see you throwing *anything* out, dear."

"It's my son," Lucille says, defensively. "He's a great believer in recycling, you see. He comes every Tuesday and carts it all off for me, God knows where."

"Doesn't give you much to do, does it." Mrs. Simmons is practically clucking her tongue in sympathy. "Never mind, dear. He means well, I'm sure."

"I want to go with you, that's all."

Robert is peering at her, not with sympathy, but with suspicion. "Why?" he asks.

"Oh, Bobby!" Miss F. says, sharply. "Your Mummy wants to come with us, that's all. What's the big deal? It'll be nice for her to get out." Lucille nearly winces at the Olive Oyl voice, and refrains from telling Miss F. that her son's name is Robert, Bob perhaps, but definitely *not* Bobby and that her, Lucille's, name is Lucille, conceivably Lucy to intimate friends, which Miss F. is not, and certainly *not* Mummy, as if she were standing there wrapped in decaying bandages. She is also resolutely ignoring Miss F's wardrobe, especially the flowered pedalpushers and plastic sandals, not to mention the orange toenails protruding from them. At least Robert looks endearingly poverty-stricken in his frayed tweed sportscoat and dull, cracked loafers—like Henry, she thinks, with a pang of tenderness, when I first met him in school.

She smiles and gestures at the neat piles of newspapers and magazines at their feet, the brown paper sack with the few tin cans she'd borrowed from Mrs. Simmons. "I'd like to see this recycling place, that's all. I'd like to see where you go every Tuesday. What's wrong?"

"You've never asked before," Robert says. "And you told me I should be looking for a job and not driving you around. You're acting funny, Ma. Mel said you were."

"Well, everyone changes, Bobby." Miss F's nasal pout has a tinge of defiance. "Your Mummy's got a right to change every now and then, doesn't she?" Lucille looks at Miss F. a little more charitably and thinks perhaps poor Miss F. suffers from adenoids. "I mean, why don't you just tie her down to a chair if you don't want her to do anything different!" Yes, Lucille decides. Adenoids.

The recycling center turns out to be not the squat cinder block construction in an industrial neighborhood Lucille had been expecting, but a quaint woodframe cottage on the outskirts of town, painted a deep green, with a meadow waving in the breeze behind it. Cheery young people in overalls and bill caps separate glass, crush cans in a hand-operated press, stack newspapers and magazines. Lucille feels slightly foolish in her carefully matched clothes, and she finds the easy smiles and exuberant energy of the place strangely stimulating. She envies the workers their worth and wants to tell Robert how happy she is to be here, but Robert has left them, muttering something about making a phone call. Miss F. watches him slouch off toward the payphone, then plucks at Lucille's sleeve. "Come on outside," she whispers, and Lucille follows her through a back door, to a bench warmed in the late afternoon sun, where they gaze out over the meadow for a few moments in silence while Miss F. rummages in her voluminous denim shoulder bag. Lucille recognizes the tightly wrapped joint that finally emerges and smolders to life. "Don't mind Bobby too much," Miss F. gasps through withheld breath. "He's not too good with things changing, people changing." Lucille hesitates only a moment before taking the joint, the smoke strong and sweet in her lungs, not at all like the acrid, irritating cigarette smoke she subjected herself to for all those years. She holds her breath, and it is as if she is poised between something ending and something beginning, a rest between movements. Miss F. is saying something further about Robert, but Lucille is watching the tall grass waving gracefully against blue sky, is feeling the warmth of the sun bathing her face, is listening to the chatter and rattle from inside the building; she is peaceful. Then she breathes out slowly, and observes to Miss F. that it's difficult being the constant in someone's life, like Henry was to her for forty-one years. "A burden," she sighs dramatically, "that's what it is," and she forgives Henry everything. They sit companionably until the joint is finished.

Back inside, Lucille smiles at the colored bits of glass spilling from the crushers, streams of liquid green and brown that will be melted and changed into new shapes for new purposes. Miss F. (No, Frankie. She will think of her as Frankie now) leads her into another room filled with displays extolling the virtues of recycling, including a jacket made from recycled bits of plastic bottles and newsprint. Frankie has taken the jacket from its display rack and is holding it up against Lucille's thin frame. "Perfect!" she honks. "You look perfect recycled!"

Robert appears while they stand there giggling, looking from one to the other, but especially at Lucille. "It's time to go home," is all he says.

"Stoned! Our seventy-one-year-old mother was standing there stoned, giggling like a schoolgirl." Robert is saying this to Melinda, both of them sitting, stern-faced, on Lucille's sofa. They look so old, Lucille is thinking, that she finds it difficult seeing them as her children. "That's not why I called you, but that's what they were doing while I was on the phone," Robert says.

Melinda glares at him. "I warned you about that Freddie person."

"Frankie," Lucille says. "Her name is Frankie, and I think she's very nice."

"A nice little drug peddler," Melinda says.

Lucille wishes Robert would defend Frankie, but he just looks away and chews his lip—another habit of Henry's, Lucille suddenly remembers.

"Shut up, Melinda," she hears herself say.

Melinda stiffens, Lucille can see it under her daughter's baggy black turtleneck and shapeless, ripped jeans, while Robert just stares. "You are not to speak to me as if I'm some helpless child. I happened to have a lovely afternoon, and that's what's bothering you. You want me to sit here like a stuffed animal in a cage, and I won't do it anymore." She is pleased with this outburst, more so at Melinda's hushed "Mother!" They stare at each other.

"Robert," Lucille says, "please go make us some coffee," and Robert shuffles gratefully out of the room.

"Do you need to talk to someone?" Melinda asks. "Someone professional, I mean. I have a friend, she has a very successful practice. I'm sure you'd like her."

"I'm sure I wouldn't." Melinda is helpless in the face of this resistance. Lucille can see it in the slump of Melinda's usually military shoulders, in the fingers picking at the threads of the ripped jeans, and for an instant Melinda is once again Henry's little girl—not Lucille's, but Henry's, that's the way it always was.

"I only want what's best for you," Melinda says quietly, and Lucille tries to think of an appropriate response, but what she is noticing is the tiny bit of blue peeking out from the cuff of Melinda's dull black coat, a blue so bright it seems to be leaking out the bottom of the coat's sleeves.

"I miss him too, you know," Lucille finally says.

They listen to Robert's clatter from the kitchen and watch the late afternoon sun retreating from the carpet, the shadows descending the walls. ✳

A PROOF FOR ROXANNA

➤ THOMAS McCONNELL

Her father had been a professor of philology and at least one evening a week all her remembered life he played the violin amid the glow of tall white tapers in silver candelabras while their guests waltzed among the lurching shadows on the wall. The party spoke three or four languages, some guests more, jokes passed back and forth, were translated from tongue to tongue and the laughter began all over again as if no pun were ever lost. But that was all before the war.

On the night after the first bombs fell, when only nine came to the flat instead of the ordinary twenty-five or thirty or once even forty-three, her father had gone into the kitchen followed by her mother and she had heard them and came in just as her father snatched the neck of their very best wine from her mother's fist and said, Irina, you know very well this is the last party.

He took the bottle back to the parlor, had everyone empty their glasses. And I will tell you a little story, he said, stooping, pouring, careful to let no drop slip.

I visited with old Chaim yesterday evening, he went on, still pouring, and all nodded for each knew the little watchsmith who had kept the neighborhood in good time for nearly seven decades, leaning over his spectacles into the ticking works. And each time I rose to leave he patted the air between us with those wonderful white hands. Where do you have to go? he said. Sit.

So I sat. We didn't talk. What was there to say. An old man is tempted to speak a good deal of nonsense at his end. But not Chaim.

He would cough and I would give him the glass from the bedside table and we would take a little water and he would cough some more and his granddaughter bless her would click the door open to see after him and I would nod and she would go out again and the silence would come back to us until the next stretch of coughing.

Once after a fit that seemed to have no stop and that finally left him retching at nothing he worked for his breath and said, You know. This night has taken years off my life.

The shadows on the wall were very still but smiles crossed the faces paled in the candlelight. The thick lens over her father's eyes glinted yellow and he coughed looking at the rug and went on without looking up.

After the all clear sounded this morning his granddaughter sent me word that he died not three hours after I left. Died at eighty-six in his own bed, fortunate man. He'll have no need of watches at long last.

A worn smile lifted her father's face, his glass lifted that they should drink.

A long silence followed. Someone murmured, That's awfully good, and then after another silence the explosions began again and came near, the closest they'd heard since the first had fallen at five-twenty that morning. Each throat caught as if only one breath were left in the room until the panes ceased shaking in the frames and then they moved as one for the stairs and the cellar.

Except her father. He went to the window and pulled aside the heavy drapes she and her mother had put up three days before for the black-out and seemed to speak to some dark body there in the night.

Krakow has the second largest open square in Europe. The Grand Square is the second largest open square in Europe, after St. Mark's in Venice. How can they bomb the second largest square in Europe?

She stood watching, waiting for him to turn, the only one to hear. Under the candles shivering on the parlor table the wine glasses shimmered nearly full of rubies. Then the siren shrilled the night into two parts. The world before sirens and the world to come.

Two mornings later her bags stood by the door waiting for Warsaw. The plan had been a train but the wireless said that all trains, even clearly marked passenger trains, were liable to be strafed from the air, so they had seats in a neighbor's car.

You know what strafe means in German? her father asked everyone, folding down the paper on the table. It means to make suffer. Let's not forget what the word means. To punish.

Her mother didn't even stop to listen anymore. She went about packing his bag on his bed while he sat unmoved with the news. From his study she called, You think we can hide behind the Carpathians forever?

Of course we can't, he said toward the door. We can no more hide behind mountains than we can hide behind history. That's precisely why I keep coming back to old Chaim's question: Where do you have to go? Where is there for a Pole to go, tell me. Every particular Pole lies pinched between the black Nazis on one side and the red Bolsheviks on the other, determined like slathering dogs to tear us in half like a sick cat. He went back to his reading. Besides, the Carpathians have already been breached.

The door opened then on her brother whose news was that there was no bread to be had for the journey. All the bakeries were closed, all the bakers called up to military service.

So we'll eat air, her father said from behind the paper.

Roxanna went to lift down his violin from the top of his closet and came to hold it toward him. When he saw, he put down the paper and lay his hand on the cracked and worn case.

There's nowhere to go, Roxanna, he sighed. But she will go to her brother's. There aren't even any mountains in Warsaw, am I not right? He shrugged. So we will all go. Then he looked up into her face. Roxanna, wherever we're going we'll have no need of this. He reached as if to touch the music a final time. Would you put it back for me, please.

Her mother came in and dropped the bag beside her father, drew her black scarf from her coat pocket, shook it out, and tying it under her chin asked what more her brother had learned outside. When he began to repeat what others were saying of the West, her father stood so that his chair trembled behind him.

France and England have no place in our geography, he said, waving the air away. The West is a myth. Then he said, Damn, and strode to his study as if recalling a deed undone. Through the opened door Roxanna saw him take up two books that lay on the desk. The Torah stayed closed in its place. She turned in time to see her mother's stare, which her mother turned on her and said, You are surprised? You know your father never goes to temple.

I heard that, he called, coming in again, the books under his arm, corners of stray manuscript escaping between their pages. I am studying to become wise. I don't need the temple for that. Put that case on the table please.

Behind pursed lips her mother shook her head and heaved up the valise.

Now we have our own democracy and we have our own choice, her father was saying, unstrapping his bag, thrusting his books among white shirts. Roxanna saw one was French and the other Latin. We can elect the godless men from the Greater German Fatherland or the godless men from Mother Russia, that's our choice.

Aren't you a godless man? her mother shouted from the hall.

Yes, he said, but I'm a Pole. That's a different world altogether.

Through the car window she saw falling planes, heard explosions that were mercifully far. It took more than two hours to leave the limits of the city. The neighbor diverged from the convoy of which they made one and kept strictly to the narrowest roads, with the consequence that they spent much of the day lost and finally gave out of benzene.

So now we'll walk to Warsaw, her father said in the last of the road dust raised by the car. She and he brought up the rear of their little column traversing the fields, making for the woods, each with one bag that they traded from hand to tired hand. Eventually, trying to circle a swamp, they surrendered even these. Her mother was crying, leaning on her brother. Her father stood weighing over his books, looking from one to the other before finally tossing both back in to the case. All he said was, Now we are stripped of our garments.

They all walked on. Twice they fell so far behind the others that her brother came back to find them and at the next rest, drinking water from stoppered bottles and watching the clouds for sounds of planes, her father told them all to go on, that he would follow in good time. I know Warsaw, he said. It's north of here.

She kept by his side despite all he reasoned until he finally shrugged. These are no shoes for fast walking, she told him and he smiled a little and laid his hand on her shoulder for a few steps. They trudged through high weeds in silence, into the needled floor of a forest of hemlocks. Towards sundown she asked him, How are you truly, Father? and he said, I have a pain, Roxanna, a terrible pain in my heart, and he tapped through his lapel with his longest finger. Here.

The others were out of sight long before the west went dark and the two of them stood before what looked a ruined outbuilding, a tumble-down lean-to against a crumbling chimney. This didn't even survive the last war, he said. She led them into its deeper dark where a battered shovel fell over and by the worn handle took a scythe to the dust with it. They slumped themselves against the stone, the rough mortar a scar at their backs. After a while she broke the quiet of the country.

So I guess this proves that you were right. All along.

Right about what?

About God.

How right?

This, she said, raised her hands to the shambles invisible in the dark surround. All this.

This proves nothing. He sighed out in the dark. One life proves nothing.

How can you say that? Here?

Let an old man finish, will you please.

She rested back her head, scratched in her hair.

One life proves something only about he who lives it, he says. Nothing more.

And yours?

Mine especially.

And what about Hitler's? About Stalin's?

Ah, he said, now we are talking about the fall of man, which began a long time ago and has always been proceeding, man by man. Only now it is a little faster. Now man falls at the speed of a dive bomber, or the speed of the bomb it drops. Once it was the speed of a fist or rock, or of a javelin. He reached from out the black pool they sat in and his hand found her knee, her hand. Or an apple. Or the jawbone of an ass. Then an arrow and then a bullet. Now a bomb. But it is the same fall. Only accelerating. Nine point eight meters per second per second. You've always known this. You don't need me to say it now.

The night, the quiet came back to them then and in it her father's head drifted down towards her own. A long long while after, just when she was ready to ask more of the darkness, she could hardly believe the snore that rattled against her, shallow and grating, not the deep sleep from the next room at home, and then as quickly the breath rasped to a halt so sudden it shook them both and dust fell from the wall behind. He had never yet said what his own life proved and that especially she wanted to know.

So she looked about her just as if she could see, tried very hard to think what she should do for them both. It should have been that everything was still in the world, waiting, in hiding, appearing dead on this night so as to survive and live a little while longer if day should come again, but the whole planet stirred round her, the leaves rustled with wind or rain, she could not know which, strange birds cried from the trees, a creature blundered low against the outer wall, blundering on. She tried again to think but on her thigh in the wreckage of her stockings some bug crawled and she twisted to pinch it between thumb and middle fingertip without disturbing her father. But already she knew he was beyond disturbing. Knew it even before she felt water run beneath her and learned that his bladder had let go. She turned to him gone stiff and when she put her lips to his cheek, cold. In a way beyond words, beyond even pictures in the mind she recognized that his soul had let go too.

As she was still saying this over to her mind a new sound invaded out in the night. Something heavy slunk the earth, not animal nor man, far but coming near. It chewed the ground and brush and dark altogether under its clank and made its own road in the world, made the wet dirt she cowered in begin to quake. A fine dust fell from the trembling above her, an old ash from the chimney she angled against. That was history again, her father would say, history approaching at the speed of a tank, and she waited now for what it would prove. *

GIRL TALK

➤ KATHRYN A. BRACKETT

"I told you, Dad, I'm not hungry."

"What about a chicken salad?" I ask.

"No."

"A cheeseburger?"

"I don't want that, either."

I'm sitting in a corner booth at Denny's with my three daughters, scrutinizing my eldest one instead of the menu in front of me. Katie has complained of a stomach ache for the last two days, nibbling on small items like oatmeal pies, soda crackers, and grapes instead of her usual double cheeseburgers and French fries. I'm wondering if she's entered that stage where all she thinks about is dieting. Does it start this early? She's only twelve.

"What about a chocolate shake?" I try again.

Katie shakes her head. Denny's is a place I know she likes, the food much better than the casserole I burned at home tonight.

"But I thought you liked them, honey?"

She pokes out her lip, and I realize my mistake. Ever since she turned eleven, she hasn't wanted me to call her honey anymore. My wife Beth once said it was a phase she would grow out of. Since Beth's death a year ago, the responsibility of understanding my daughters inside and out has switched to me. I'm an architect by profession. People pay me to construct life from nothing or to recondition the old into something new, but I can't look at a blueprint of my girls' lives and say, "Yes, right here is the problem. I can fix that."

I notice Katie looking out the window. Street lamps brighten sidewalks covered in red and orange leaves. It's only six-thirty in the evening, but the South Carolina sky is already a blackboard because of autumn. Beth liked to run at night. She'd do a few quick miles, always sticking to streets with plenty of light. She avoided sidewalks because they impaired her running. Even when she jogged close to the curb, I worried about drivers not seeing her.

I scan the menu, trying to find something appealing to Katie.

"I know what I want, Daddy!" my five-year-old says, pointing to a glossy picture of a grilled cheese basket with fries. Her name is Jillian, but we call her Jilly. She's still smiling in spite of everything that has happened.

"Okay, honey," I say. "If that's what you want."

"I have to go to the bathroom," Katie says, pushing at Megan, my ten-year old, from the inside of the booth.

"Are you okay?" I ask.

Katie scrunches up her face in irritation. It was always easier for her to talk to her mother. She rushes away from the table on tall gangly legs, shoulders high, her head slightly down. Of my three daughters, she looks the most like Beth, even though she has my tangled brown hair and not the loose auburn curls Jilly and Megan inherited from their mother.

"Do you know what's wrong with your sister?" I ask Megan.

Megan shrugs and focuses her attention on the list of food, trying to make a decision. She will read everything on the menu. She is my patient child, the meticulous one, and slightly shyer than the others. I think grief is taking its time to catch up with her, but one day I suspect she will be where Katie is now—wanting to disconnect the feelings, and angry that she can't.

I sigh and lean back in the booth. A brown-haired woman with bifocals stares at me from a table across the room. At first I think she's flirting, but then a soft expression lifts on her face, a familiar look that I understand not as pity but as a kind of admiration.

"It's a woman thing," Beth told me once when I asked her why women stared when I was out with my girls. "There's just something about seeing a man by himself with his children. It brings out an emotion in us."

Katie walks back to the table, her fingertips doing funny circles on her stomach. Megan shuffles out of the booth to let her sister in.

"Does your side hurt?" I ask Katie.

"No. Why?"

"Just thinking about your appendix."

She rolls her eyes.

"So it's not your appendix then?"

"Please stop asking me questions."

Jilly points to an ice cream sundae from the dessert menu sitting on the table. "Can I have this too!" she squeals. I run my hand through the curls that spiral down her back. Her hair is too long, but she won't let me cut it. She says she wants to grow it like Pocahontas.

"Not until you've eaten your dinner."

"But I want it now!"

Jilly seems to have been born stubborn. I've had to learn not to bow to her demands, which I did when Beth was on the receiving end. I pull Jilly onto my lap, clamping my arms around her waist, underneath the tutu pulled over her jeans. Her first dance recital is in a few days, and she refuses to take off her tutu until it's over. She's worn it for two weeks now. The only time I'm allowed to remove it is during a bath.

Allison, our waitress, comes to the table and distributes four glasses of water. "Have ya'll decided on what you'd like to eat?"

"I just need one more minute," Megan says.

Allison nods, then smiles at Jilly. "You're such a pretty ballerina," she says.

"I can spin like a butterfly way up into the air! Wanna see?"

"Honey, I'm sure this nice lady has other—"

"Oh, no. I don't mind." Allison steps aside as my daughter springs out of my arms. Jilly pushes a nearby chair out of her way, then stands in the middle of the carpeted floor, rubbing her feet back and forth to warm up. She often does this at home, having fun with static electricity afterwards by shocking her sisters.

Jilly pulls her arms above her head into the shape of a cone and twirls as fast as she can. Her curls spring along her back and fall into her face as she spins, never losing her balance. When she bows, we all clap. Even Katie, despite her mood, joins in.

Allison runs a hand over the back of Jilly's head. "You're the best ballerina I've ever seen in my life," she says.

Jilly wiggles her hips, screams, "I know!" then crawls back onto my lap. She tells Allison what she wants to eat. The waitress jots down her order, then proceeds to get the rest of ours. Before she walks away, I add a chicken salad and milkshake to the order.

Katie's face tightens.

"Honey, you have to get something in your stomach."

"I ate today."

"When?"

She pauses too long.

"My point exactly."

She folds her arms across her chest and leans back against the booth. Then she leans in close to Megan and starts whispering, girl talk that I'm not supposed to hear.

Still waiting for our food twenty minutes later, I ask Megan if she's enjoying the new Harry Potter book I bought her a few days ago. She reads voraciously.

"I've got about thirty pages left," Megan answers.

"Wow, must be a good one, huh?"

She shakes her head, then looks down and pulls at her left ear. Something's up. She only does that when she has something important to say that she thinks I won't like.

Megan focuses on me and clears her throat. "Daddy, this boy from school asked me to the harvest dance," she says fast. Then she pauses and glances at Katie, who gives her a look that says: *Go on.* "And I'd like to go with him, if that's okay with you."

I can only formulate fragments of thought: *A boy. A dance. A first. Not even had this talk with Katie yet.*

"Daddy, did you hear me?"

"How old is he?"

"Katie's age."

A twelve-year-old boy wants to take my ten-year-old daughter to a dance? Did I hear that right?

"What's his name?"

"Chase."

A twelve-year-old boy named Chase, who'll probably put his name to use, wants to take my ten-year-old daughter to a dance?

"Do you even like boys?" I ask.

"Aren't I supposed to?"

"I mean, you don't think they're nasty or something?"

"No, Daddy, she thinks he's really cute!" Jilly pipes up.

Megan shoots her sister a mean look.

"Honey, what does Chase do?"

"What do you mean? He's twelve."

"I mean, does he play sports? Does he make good grades? How does he get around?"

"Well," she says, "he has a nice bike." She says this so seriously that I can't help but laugh. I envision Chase pedaling up a hill, sweat beading on his forehead with Megan seated behind him, the ends of her dress pinned to her knees so it doesn't get caught in the spokes.

"Are you nervous about this dance?" I ask.

Megan turns pink. She stares at her hands, lightly massaging her fingers. That's all the answer I need.

"I guess it'll be all right," I say. "But I have to meet him first, okay?"

Megan's soft dimples dig into her cheeks as she smiles. Katie elbows her in happiness. And instead of enjoying this moment, I think back to when Megan was four and I flushed her fish, Sparkle, down the toilet after he died. Megan had never screamed so loud. I tried to calm her, but in the end she had turned to Beth, curling into her lap and listening as Beth told her a story about how a fish like hers had to move through a special tunnel in order to reach a magical ocean where all the sea creatures talked to each other.

"What do they talk about?" Megan had asked.

Beth held her close. "They chat about little girls like you and how much they loved them." Megan had settled against Beth while I stood in the doorway, watching. Now, from the rosiness in Megan's cheeks, I can tell she's excited about the dance, thinking about what she'll wear, what she'll say to Chase when they're alone, what she might do, God forbid, if he tries to kiss her—feelings she thinks I know nothing about because I'm her father. And then something turns inside me. What if he does try to kiss her?

"You know, Megan, I think you're a little young for dating," I say. "Let me think about it."

"But you just told her she could go," Katie blurts.

"I changed my mind."

"You can't do that."

"I didn't say no. I just said I needed to think about it."

"You're being unfair," Katie presses on. "It's just a dance. What could happen?"

"*A lot* could happen."

Both Katie and Megan roll their eyes at me. I wonder if the gesture is somehow contagious.

I breathe a sigh of relief when Allison brings our food to the table. Jilly pushes out of my lap and back into her booster seat as soon as the grilled cheese basket is in front of her. Allison places a huge glass in front of Katie. "And here's your milkshake, dear."

"I don't want it."

The waitress shifts her attention to me. "Did I mess up ya'll's order?"

"It's fine," I say. "Thank you." Allison walks away. I focus on Katie. "Honey, does your stomach hurt that much?"

"I don't know."

"How could you not know?"

"Dad, quit bugging me!"

I stare at her, hurt by the tone of her voice. "Honey, I only care—"

"Jilly, you're so gross!" Megan suddenly yells. My eyes drop to Jilly as she sinks her right hand into the red-middle of her French fries, hunting for them through a mass of ketchup I've inadvertently let her pour for herself.

"Don't eat like that," I scold, reaching for a napkin. "You know better."

"I've got to go to the bathroom." Katie shoves Megan and runs across the room.

Allison rounds a corner with a pitcher of water. I rush up to her. "Would you mind going into the bathroom to check on Katie?" I ask. "It's her stomach. I'm not really sure what's wrong. I would do it, but I have to watch my other—"

"Daddy!"

Megan's urgent bellow gets my attention. I spin around, see her pointing at Jilly. "Make her stop! She's grossing me out!"

"Shut up, Megan!" Jilly yells.

"You shut up!"

I turn back to Allison.

"Don't worry, sir," she says calmly. "I'll check on your daughter."

I cross the room and slide into the booth just as Jilly throws a limp French fry at Megan. I smack her hand. She lowers her eyes, kicks at the booth, then slyly lifts her gaze and sticks out her tongue at Megan. I don't have time to scold her, because Allison walks up to tell me Katie is crying in the bathroom.

"Did she tell you what's wrong?"

She speaks slowly, offers a gentle smile. "Yes, she did, but I think you should talk to her." I look at Jilly and Megan. "Don't worry, I'll watch them," she adds.

As I walk away, Allison cheers, "I've got some toys for you!"

I scurry around a "wet floor" sign in front of the bathroom, walk inside, and hear Katie in the stall closest to the sink.

I knock on the door. "Katie, honey, are you okay?"

"Oh, jeez, Dad!" she says in a tear-filled voice. "Men aren't supposed to be in here!"

I hear toilet paper rolling. Sniffles. More toilet paper.

"Honey, what's wrong?"

"You won't understand."

"Let me be the judge of that."

Katie steps out of the stall, her face red from crying. She looks me straight in the eyes and says, "I started my period." The whole ground seems to tip sideways. I open my mouth, but nothing comes out. "I don't know what to do," she adds, looking at me for an answer.

I rub the back of my neck, cross my arms in front of my chest, shift my weight to another foot, then say, "Well … that is … quite an accomplishment, honey."

"Jeez, Dad! I never should have told you!" Katie races back into the stall and locks it.

My head spins. I collect myself, breathe deep, knock on the door. "I'm sorry, Katie. Please come out, or else I'm crawling under."

"Promise you won't act funny?"

"I quadruple promise."

The door clicks open. Katie's bangs flutter into her eyes, mixing with the tears stuck to her lashes. I glance at the box on the wall that holds the feminine products. It looks like a large candy machine to me.

"Do you need some money for a … a pad or tampon, well, maybe not a tampon, maybe that's too much for you now, but—"

"Dad."

"Sorry." I fumble in my pocket for loose change, handing her two dollars in quarters. She takes the money but doesn't move.

"Is that not enough?" I ask. "Because I have more."

Her face reddens. "No, it's more than enough."

"Do you know … how to … put a pad on?"

"Yes," she says, her mouth full of the word. "I'll figure it out."

"Oh, good. Good."

She stays quiet for so long that I wonder if there's something more I should do.

"Are you in pain?" I ask, remembering Beth's discomfort every month.

"A little."

"Maybe I'll order you some hot tea. That always helped your mother."

And that does it. Katie starts sobbing all over again.

I get down on one knee, reach out to her. I know she says, "I don't know what to do without Mama," but what I hear between her sobs is: "I duun … no whutdo witout Ma … ma."

My breath catches in my throat. She cried hard like this at Beth's funeral, right into the center of my chest. All I could do then was hold her tight and reassure her that somehow things would be okay. I wish I could ball up all her pain and hold it inside me.

I touch her shoulders, feel myself relax. "I didn't realize you were old enough for this big step," I say. "But this is a good thing. It might not seem like that now, but it really is." I rub tears from her eyes with the pad of my thumb. She doesn't stop me.

"Mama always said that I could start as early as ten."

"What else did she tell you?"

"She said it would be something really special when it happened, and that because of it, I'll be like an oyster where the best pearls will grow inside me one day."

Beth would have said that. She wouldn't have told me about the conversation, either. It would have been their secret, something for me to know only when it was time.

"Your mama's right," I say.

The door flies open and the brown-haired woman with the bifocals steps inside. She stops when she sees me, glances at the label on the door then looks me up and down. "How in the Sam Hill did you get in here?"

"Sorry, ma'am," I say. "I'm just taking care of my daughter. I'm leaving now." I look to Katie. "I'll see you back at the table."

She nods, her face gleaming with a spark of confidence that I hope will deepen as she grows.

When I leave the bathroom and slide into the booth, Jilly is shoving spoonfuls of chocolate ice cream into her mouth and Megan is carefully scraping whipped cream from her banana nut sundae onto a napkin.

"Why do you always order whipped cream if you don't want it?" I ask.

"Because sometimes I change my mind." She pauses. "Just like you." She sulks over her ice cream, eating all the nuts off the top.

"You know, Megan, the trick to getting over your nerves for a dance is to practice some steps with your old man." She straightens up, the miffed look on her face slowly fading. "You'll be the best dancer on the floor," I tell her. "Chase won't know what hit him."

She watches me a moment, one curious brow arched. "You really mean it?"

"Maybe we'll have him over for dinner tomorrow night for some fried chicken."

Her lips curl into a wide smile, and deep within hers I imagine she's screaming: Yes!

Katie joins us a few minutes later. She sips her milkshake, though it's soupy now. I remember that's the way she likes it. She exchanges a comfortable look with me, and for the first time all day she doesn't look like she feels unwell. I check on Megan beside her, then Jilly. All my girls seem satisfied for once.

Every night I slip into their rooms and watch them sleep. I see them cuddled in their beds: Katie with the covers half-off, Megan with them pulled up close to her neck, Jilly with them twisted all around her legs. When I watch my girls in those quiet hours of sleep, breathing in their own rhythmic pace, the pain of losing Beth doesn't take so much out of me. I can keep going then. I can keep breathing, as long as my daughters are listening somewhere nearby. *

PRETTY PITIFUL GOD

➤ DENO TRAKAS

I didn't know it was Jack Kerouac—I just thought it was some drunk who'd passed out on his lawn after a night of drinking. I guess it was both.

I was roofing for the summer, 1969, St. Petersburg, Florida. I was sixteen, didn't even have a draft card, and it was my first real job, and pretty damn hard, especially the heavy heat and those big ballsy afternoon thunderstorms that blast and boom and cool you off for about ten minutes then steam you pink. But the money was good, $3 an hour.

We were working on a house on Tenth Avenue North, and I'd just climbed up onto one of those Spanish tile roofs you see all over Florida, and there, in the back yard of the house next door, lay a man, flat on his back with his arms out like Jesus, in an untucked blue flannel shirt— flannel in summer, I swear—and rumpled pants with the fly unzipped, as if he'd come outside to take a piss and the effort wore him out.

His dark hair was shaggy but not long like a hippie's, and his face was unshaved, and he was either dead or asleep. I called to my boss, "Jerry, come look at this."

Jerry got up and crossed the roof, which, like most in Florida, didn't have much pitch at all. I pointed at the body. "Is he dead?" Jerry asked.

"I don't think so. I think I saw his eye twitch."

"Looks dead, if you axe me. I'll check it out," he said. He climbed down the ladder and returned in a few minutes, during which time the body didn't move. "I axed the woman here and she says it's the guy who owns that house. Says he used to own this one. Name's Kerouac. Used to be famous or something. Now he's just a drunk. She said she'd call his wife, and we shouldn't worry about him."

"Jack Kerouac?"

"Yeah, I think that's what she said."

"No way. I've read his books. He's my hero. He's like God."

"Pretty pitiful god, if you axe me. Let's get back to work."

I climbed down to get another load of tiles, but I kept my eye on Kerouac, and in a while, a stout, dark-haired, middle-aged woman, dressed in fuzzy slippers and a muumuu, came out and tried to rouse him. She bent over him, spoke softly, and patted his face. After a minute, his eyes jerked open, he slapped her hand away and snapped at her, words I couldn't hear but whose snarly tone was clear enough. She stood up straight, said something back, and went inside. He lay there for at least another fifteen minutes, eyes squinted as if he were trying to read the want ads in the clouds, but finally he staggered to his feet and wobbled into his house.

For the rest of the day I thought about those guys in *On the Road* and how much they drank and screwed and did whatever the hell they wanted and how there never seemed to be consequences, or at least not permanent consequences, because if you got drunk or stoned you could sleep it off; if you were broke you could steal or get a whatever job for a while; if you had a friend, you always had a place to go, even if he abandoned you in Mexico or stole your girl; if you tried everything and dug everything, you never got bored; and if you kept moving, you never got stuck in a rut—that's what *On the Road* meant to me. It was wild and fun and proof that you didn't have to grow up to be a barber. But now this. Jack Kerouac, the king of cool, just an old man the same age as my old man, passed out flat on his back in the backyard of a little house, a lot like my own house, here in nowhere St. Pete.

The next day Kerouac wasn't there in the grass, but he came over during our lunch break, found us sitting in the thin shade of some pine trees, listening to a rock radio station, eating our sandwiches and drinking Coke from our thermoses. He looked sober and showered, sturdy and pot-bellied, and carried a paper plate of something covered with aluminum foil. "I brought you knaves some baklava. My wife makes the best in town." He handed the plate to Jerry.

"Thanks," Jerry said as he lifted the foil and examined the strange parallelograms of pastry.

"They're Greek, filo and honey from the descendants of Athena herself."

Jerry said thanks again, took one, and passed them around.

Kerouac said, "My neighbor tells me there's a fan among you."

After a second I realized he must be talking about me, so I said, "Yes, sir, that's me."

He nodded. "What's your name, son?"

"Wayne, Wayne Hollis."

"Well, Wayne Hollis, as far as I know, you're my only roofer fan. I'm pleased to know you." He held out his hand, but I'd just picked up a piece of baklava and my fingers were sticky, so I had to wipe them on my pants first. Then I tried to get up, but he said not to, and we shook, him standing, me sitting. "It's an honor, Mr. Kerouac."

"Jack. Call me Jack. Can I get you men anything else? Water or Cokes or a little Sartre?"

I'd heard of Sartre, at least I knew he was a writer, and I thought that was pretty funny, but we all just shook our heads and did a round of no thanks.

"All right, then. Carry on. I don't know how you do it in this heat—I admire you." And with that he nodded again and left us. Maybe he was going next door to write another great book.

"Nice guy," Jerry said. "There's no man so nice as a drunk when he's sober, if you axe me."

I didn't know any drunks, at least I didn't know they were drunks if they were, but Jerry's reasoning seemed about right. Still, I was impressed with the stand-up Kerouac, a famous man who'd brought us dessert and singled me out, and I couldn't wait to tell Ferg.

"This pastry thing is good," one of my co-workers said, "but it's going to make me thirsty as hell. Anybody want the rest of it?" We shook our heads, so he threw the half-eaten baklava into the bushes, which made me sad.

My dad had been the head barber at Webb City, a huge store downtown where you could get a fast haircut, buy your groceries, and then go upstairs to see the sexy mermaid show. An ambitious, wacky place, but it was somehow out of synch with the sixties, and when it started to fold, my dad bailed and opened a little shop a few blocks away, where he snipped the thin hair of old men and struggled to pay the bills. I didn't hate him for being a barber, or for anything else, but he was real uptight, and the house was uptight, five of us squeezed into three bedrooms and one bathroom, without air conditioning, and it was all about money. I remember that in seventh grade I had one button-down collar shirt with a fruit loop that I really liked, and I wore it almost every day until one of my friends told me it stunk and asked me if I didn't have another one, which I didn't.

We had a Chevy station wagon, which my dad drove—he dropped me off at work, but otherwise I had to catch rides with friends or take the bus or walk. When I picked up my first paycheck, I started thinking about buying a car. It was a practical thing, but the inspiration could've come from Kerouac—that Hudson that Dean drove back and forth across the country like four-door freedom.

Some nights my dad would let me use his car if I told him where I was going and came home by curfew, and Ferg talked me into taking him over to meet Kerouac. I didn't really want to—I mean, who were we to show up at Jack Kerouac's door?—but Ferg was so hip on the idea that he just wouldn't let go of it. So we drove over, and as we headed up the front walk, I hoped nobody would be home, even though there were lights on inside and music playing on a hi-fi. At the door, Ferg was hopping from foot to foot and saying, "I can't believe this, man, this is so cool."

The woman answered, dressed in the same muumuu as before. She said "Yes," as if she would agree to whatever we asked.

I said, "Hi, I'm one of the guys who works on the roof next door, and this is my friend, and, well, he wanted to meet Mr. Kerouac, if it wouldn't be too much trouble."

"Just a minute," she said with a faint accent and closed the door enough so that we couldn't look inside.

Ferg kept jabbering and jittering, and I told him to stop or Kerouac would think he was an idiot, which he wasn't—Ferg was probably going to M.I.T. in a year—but he couldn't hold still. In a couple of minutes,

Kerouac opened the door, red-eyed, heavy-lidded and sluggish, wearing a t-shirt, wrinkled pants, no shoes, like he'd just gotten up from a nap in the back yard. "Evenin' boys," he said. "What can I do you for?"

I expected Ferg to burst into expressions of adoration, but his face was stuck in a ridiculous grin and he was obviously tongue-tied with awe, so I said, "Sorry to bother you, Mr. Kerouac, but my friend here wanted to meet you. His name's Dave Ferguson, but we call him Ferg."

I thought he'd step outside, shake our hands, and shoot the breeze for a few minutes, but instead he said, "You boys have a car?"

"Yes, sir," I said.

"You have any money?"

I thought these were weird questions, but I answered, "A couple of bucks." Then he and I both looked at Ferg, who nodded his goofy grin.

"I'll be right out," he said and closed the door.

Now Ferg and I looked at each other. I said, "Does this mean he's going out with us?"

Ferg nodded. "I can't believe it, man. This is so cool. This is like the best day of my life."

"Where will we go?" I asked.

"It doesn't matter, man, we're going out with Jack Kerouac."

And we did. He came out buttoning his lumberjack shirt and said "Vamonos," so we got in the station wagon and he told me where to go. On the way we didn't talk much because he had to concentrate on his navigation, which was confused and made me suspect that he'd already been drinking. Eventually we ended up in a bar in Pinellas Park where the bartender and some of the customers greeted Kerouac by name. It was about nine-thirty, still early by bar standards, I guess, so there were some empty booths and Kerouac told us to claim one. We did and in a few minutes he joined us, awkwardly stuffing himself in beside Ferg. "The night is immense, boys." He said it slowly and sadly, so I guessed an immense night was a bad thing, but then some jazzy music started playing from a jukebox, and a waitress brought over a pitcher of beer and three mugs. She winked at me as she filled my glass, then she wiggled off in her miniskirt and fishnet stockings. I didn't know if the wink meant that she knew I was underage or that she thought I was cute, but hell, I didn't care, even if she was old, over thirty.

To quote Ferg, I couldn't believe it, man. I'd never even been in a bar, much less flirt with a waitress and share a pitcher of beer with Jack Kerouac in a bar. I felt like the coolest dude in the city, and I wished the girls at school could see me now.

Kerouac turned to Ferg, who had a mustache of foam over his lip from his first sip of beer, and said, "What'd you say your name was?"

"Dave Ferguson."

"Oh yeah, Ferg of St. Petersburg. You look like Lucien, an old friend of mine. You haven't killed anybody, have you?"

"No," Ferg spluttered.

"Lucien did. A guy who was following him around."

"Really?"

"You don't have a knife on you, do you?"

"No."

"I helped him get rid of the knife and had to spend a week in jail for being an accessory. I had to get married to get out of jail."

"Wow. Are you serious?"

"I thought you'd read my books."

"I have. I've read em all."

"No you haven't. *Visions of Gerard, Doctor Sax, Maggie Cassidy, Vanity of Duluoz, Visions of Cody, Tristessa* ... I could go on." He listed his books crisply, but bored, like a waiter at a fancy restaurant telling us the specials.

Well, maybe not all of them." Ferg dropped his head, disappointed in himself.

Kerouac draped his arm over Ferg's shoulder and said, "It's OK, son, nobody's read em all. According to my royalty checks, no one's reading anything I've written." The arm lingered there as if to console them both, then came down.

"But that can't be true. You've got thousands of fans."

"Used to, maybe, but fame is a whore, boys—if you don't pay, she don't put out."

I'd never heard an adult, or anybody, talk like that, so I didn't know what to say. I just nodded, in a knowing way, as if that had been my experience too, and sipped my beer. He finished his glass and, with trembling hands, poured another. Ferg was trying to keep up with him, but was half a glass behind, but at least his tongue had been untied. "Have you really done all those things in your books, Mr. Kerouac?"

"Jack, call me Jack, and yeah, they're pretty straight, much to the chagrin of some of my friends. All the names are changed to protect the guilty."

I kept thinking he was funny, but he never smiled and seemed sad, deep sad.

"Man, I'd be flattered if someone wrote about me," Ferg said.

"Maybe I will," Kerouac said. "Are you interesting?"

"No."

Kerouac looked at me and asked, "Is he interesting?"

"No," I said. "Neither of us is. Not like you."

"Oh, I bet there's a lot more story in you than you think. We could commandeer that old station wagon of yours out there and flap a mattress in the back and take off for Frisco right now, and you'd be just like Sal and Dean."

We both smiled, and Ferg said, "Man, that would be so cool."

"So let's go," Kerouac said and finished off his second glass of beer and smacked the mug down on the table like a decision.

Ferg and I looked at each other for clues as to how to read this. Surely he was just pulling our legs, but he looked and sounded serious.

"Nah, we can't. It's not my car," I said.

"Did you steal it?" Kerouac asked.

"It's my dad's."

"If you took it, what would he do?"

"I don't know."

"What if you called him from another state, told him everything was copacetic?"

"What does that mean?"

"Cool, fine, satisfactory."

"He wouldn't send the cops," Ferg said. "He'd let you go. My dad, on the other hand, would send the cops and the FBI and the marines, and he'd beg them to throw me in the slammer."

Kerouac leaned back and closed his eyes, obviously bored with his unadventurous sidekicks and their adolescent conversation. Ferg and

I just looked at each other, like now what? Kerouac said, "You hear that?"

It was a saxophone solo, moaning from the jukebox. "Man, that's cool," Ferg said.

"It's profound," Kerouac said. "That tenorman's wringing the grief right out of the night."

"That's good," I said. I meant the music was good, even though I wasn't really a jazz fan, and his description was good. "How do you do that? How do you make up lines like that?"

With his trembling hand he poured his third glass and topped off ours, emptying the pitcher. He shook his head. "Music's all about ideas and feelings, so that's the way you have to describe it." Janis Joplin came on after the sax solo, and Kerouac tilted his head and tutored us some more. "Now that's fear—she's like a Commie on the loose in the U.S. of A. with so much freedom she has to scream."

I almost understood him, even though he sounded political and I was feeling mystical; but then he broke it up, saying "Where'd that bitch go?" I thought he was talking about Janis Joplin, but then he yelled, "We need another pitcher over here."

Just about everyone in the bar turned to look, and I was embarrassed. The barmaid came over, cocked her big hip, fixed Kerouac a disapproving glare and said, "Now don't get started, Jack. You remember what happened last time."

"Just trying to be a good host to these young men, Betty." She hmmmphed and took the pitcher. As the air warmed back up behind her, he asked, "You boys have girlfriends?"

We both shook our heads and Ferg said, "No."

"Really? Couple a good looking boys and you're not getting laid?"

"We wish," I said.

"What's the problem?"

"Girls," I said.

He didn't laugh as I thought he would but said, in a dreamy voice, "They're snakes, but remember, they're just as afraid of you as you are of them. You gotta be bold, even if you're pissin your pants."

"How do you do that?" Ferg asked.

He concentrated and looked from me to Ferg seriously. "Respect the soul, listen to it, the beat of the blood in your veins—that's where all rhythm comes from, you know—it'll lift you up and make you a god."

I didn't know what that had to do with girls, but I didn't want to ask and sound stupid so I just nodded my head. Ferg said, "The girls we know don't listen to the soul. They'd just laugh at us."

"Sometimes you need an older person to show you the way."

Did he mean he'd give us tips, or did he mean we should look for older girls, or women like the barmaid, who happened to show up at that moment with another full pitcher? He said thank you, and she said you're welcome, and she smiled, and I thought everything was copacetic. But as Jack filled his glass he said, "Betty, these boys wanta lose their cherries. You wantem?"

I'd never heard the phrase, but I guessed its meaning and blushed and wouldn't look at her. But I could tell she was looking at me, amused. "Call me when you're legal, big boy," she said, pinched my cheek, and sashayed away.

Kerouac laughed for the first time, drank half his glass, and said, noticeably slurring a word or two, "I was jus like you. SSStill in high school, moonin over pretty girls, ssscared to make a move. You boys beat off?"

That wasn't something I talked about, to anyone, not even my friends. I looked at Ferg, who was equally mortified.

Kerouac put his arm around Ferg again and said, "S'okay, boys, you wouldn't be normal if you didn't. Y'ever get a blow job?"

My God! I remembered the first time I saw a picture of a woman giving a man a blow job, how gross and silly it looked, and I hadn't learned anything since to change my opinion. Ferg took a big gulp of beer and shook his head, and I said "No" firmly enough for both of us.

"I like blow jobs," he said. "They're like a good blow on a horn, y'know, they're pure, they're e-sssen-tial. I can ssshow you how if you want."

He said it offhandedly, like he wanted to show me how to shoot a hook shot or something, so it took a minute for me to understand the nature of the proposition. Then I was scared. Part of me wanted to say to Ferg, Let's get the hell outa here. But the rest of me, the obedient boy, wouldn't let me be disrespectful to an adult, especially a famous one. So I just sat up straight and said, "No thanks."

Kerouac looked at Ferg, shrinking under the lumberjack arm, and said, "Howboutyou?"

Ferg just shook his head, fast.

"S'allright. I'm not a fag if tha's what you're thinkin. It's jus, nothin wrong with homoeroticism. Everything's the Holy Ghost."

I had no idea what the hell he was talking about now. And didn't care. I just wanted to go home, and I looked at my watch.

Kerouac noticed and said, "S'cool, boys. Drink up. We got plenny beer and the night's a pearl and we're jus crackin the ssshell."

My glass was about half full, and I knew that if I drank it fast, I'd start to wobble, which was usually my goal but was now my excuse. "This'll be it for me. I've got to drive."

Ferg said idiotically, "Me too."

"C'mon boys. Le's finish this n we can go to a jazz club, I know one ona beach where a big black cat plays ethereal bass, I mean e-THER-eal, you'll dig 'im. N we can go out ona beach n watch the moon rise, like a ball-headed Lazarus, n we'll be alive again, n we can ssswim to Mexico, you'll DIG Mexico." He drained his glass and refilled it.

I studied him: Kerouac was older than my dad, and dark and serious and speaking metaphors, and he wanted us to stay with him—why was that? —didn't he have any grown-up friends? —was he still hoping for a blow job? And here we were, two kids wanting adventure, we thought, wanting to be just like him, we thought, but now we just wanted to go home.

"I'm sorry, Mr. Kerouac," I said, "but I gotta go to work in the morning. I gotta climb a ladder with a hundred pounds of tiles on my shoulder."

"Me too," Ferg said again, still being an idiot, which made me like him more than ever.

"S'allright. S'fine. 'Nother time. I'll go on home to m'wife and mother."

He didn't sound like he was being sarcastic. "You live with your wife and mother?" I asked, unable to hide the surprise in my voice, remembering the woman in the muumuu.

"Yeah, you gotta problem w'that?"

"No, I think it's fine, nice, copacetic."

"My mother worked in a ssshoe fact'ry to s'port me and put up w'all kinds of ssshit. S'least I can do. An my wife …"

"I admire it," I said, and I did, as if I'd discovered a new facet on this worn gem. And I wasn't afraid anymore. But I still wanted to go. "As soon as you finish your beer, I'll take you home."

He guzzled it like I guzzled water in the middle of the afternoon on a hot roof. He seemed resigned and disappointed that we weren't the companions, co-conspirators, or saviors he had hoped we might be, and I felt that I had failed some kind of test. Then he yelled to Betty, scribbled wildly in the air, and she brought us the bill. Ferg and I had just enough to cover it, which was a good thing because Kerouac said he was broke.

And it was a good thing I knew how to get to his house because he crawled into the back of the station wagon and passed out or fell asleep. When we arrived, we tried to wake him but ended up carrying him to the door—he was heavy. The woman in the muumuu showed us in and pointed to a sofa where we laid him out.

That roofing job was over in a couple of days, and Kerouac never appeared in that time. Ferg and I read more of his stuff and talked about him and wondered if we could be writers and tried to listen to our souls, but all I ever heard was my stomach rumbling.

I turned seventeen. I got a crush on a cute, smart girl who worked with me on the yearbook staff, and I asked her to homecoming. She agreed, and I depleted my car savings in order to buy some new clothes, including a cool leather vest and some corduroy bell bottoms. We dated for a few weeks, and I didn't score, but I got to third base because that's where she wanted me, and I was happy to have gotten that far.

About that time, one morning Ferg ran up to me at my locker and said, "Did you hear?" And I said "What?" And he said, "Kerouac died, man. A hemorrhage or something."

We went to the open casket service at a funeral home across town, Ferg and I, and looked down at the famous face that was clean-shaven, grayer and thinner and handsomer than when we'd met him, more serene too. There were almost no visitors, which was sad enough, but there was the woman in the muumuu, now wearing a black dress, standing somberly behind a wheelchair in which sat an old lady crying, blubbering, "Oh my little boy … Isn't he pretty? … What will I do now?"

But that's not how I remember Kerouac. I remember him lying flat on his back in the grass, looking up at me, I'm on his roof, and cumulus clouds are boiling up behind me, as if God has taken to chain smoking because his people make him nervous. Kerouac waves and smiles because his roof needs fixing, and I'm going to get it done before it rains. *

TRUTH GAME

> ➤ MARILYN KNIGHT

"Maggie! *Maggie,* where are you?"

Maggie Rouse, tucked into a hollow between low dunes, lifted her head and watched Ashton Corbin walk down the steps of the weathered beach cottage. Under a low, gray sky Ashton's blonde hair was the only spot of brightness.

Maggie glanced down at the book cradled on her knees: *A Wrinkle in Time*. It was her favorite lately, and she was just getting to the best part, when Meg finally saves Charles Wallace. She considered remaining hidden, her cropped brown hair and faded sweatshirt blended into the dull scenery. But she'd read the book three times since school let out for the summer, and her mother would be mad and sad if she found out Maggie was hiding from Ashton.

Wearing her new leopard-print bikini, Ashton was crossing the patch of yard that gave way to the dunes. She cupped her hands around her mouth, careful to avoid her shiny lip gloss and called again, "Maggie!"

"Here I am." She stood up, brushing sand off the seat of her shorts. Why was Ashton wearing a swimsuit? She hated to get wet, and she didn't care much for the beach either, except to lie on it in a sun-drugged stupor, coated in tanning oil, iPod in ear and Blackberry in hand. There was no sun today. The wind off the ocean was chilly, and it was beginning to spit rain.

"Let's walk down to Grogan's and get a Coke," Ashton called. That explained it. Ashton had a crush on the boy, Tim or Tom or something, who worked at Grogan's Store, selling bait and candy and soft drinks.

"The refrigerator's full of Cokes," Maggie said, making her way out of the sand and into the yard. "Let's do something else. We could walk down the beach and look for sand dollars."

"Oh, don't be so boring," Ashton pouted, tilting her head. Her hair hung down her back in streaky yellow waves. She'd been a blonde toddler, but her hair had turned sandy brown, almost as dark as Maggie's as she'd gotten older. The heavy streaks were new this summer, and Maggie saw that she had painted her fingernails metallic gold and wore glittery gold eye shadow. Ridiculous. Maggie curled her bitten nails into her palms. Ridiculous, a girl that age. That's what her father had said about Ashton's bleached hair and all the makeup she wore.

"Come on, Maggie, let's go to Grogan's. I want a Pepsi, not a Coke." She linked her arm with Maggie's, pulling her along. "I don't want to go by myself."

Maggie allowed herself to fall into step with Ashton. It wasn't easy. Her head came just above Ashton's shoulder, which wasn't fair. They both were twelve, but Maggie had just had her birthday, and Ashton would be thirteen in August. Ashton already filled out the top of her bikini and had long, tanned legs. She also had white Ray Bans and a little leopard-print skirt to tie over her bikini—to hide her big butt. Maggie tried not to hate her.

"Give it a chance, Maggie," her mother had said back in the spring. "It'll be fun, just us four girls, hanging out at the beach all summer. You'll see. We'll swim, we'll shop, we'll go into Charleston and sightsee. You know we always have a great time at Aunt Peg's. Besides, how can we turn down a whole summer at the beach?"

There were lots of things Maggie could have said in reply, but didn't. Like how her mother was the only one who really had a good time during the week or so that their family spent each summer on Sullivan's Island with Dan and Peggy Corbin and their darling Ashton.

Aunt Peg and her mother had grown up together, been college roommates, and still talked on the phone at least once a week. Actually, for the past few months it had been more like once a day, starting back in the fall when Dan and Peggy had separated. Peggy was asking for the house in Columbia, the beach cottage, and lots of child support.

"Fifteen thousand a month, plus the house, *and* the beach house? Kay, he inherited that beach cottage from his grandfather, for Christ's sake," Maggie's father had said.

"He's a plastic surgeon, Max. That kind of money is nothing to him. Besides, Peg deserves everything she can get." Her mother had slammed the door as she'd walked away.

Maggie's father taught history at the university, and every year he'd argued for a vacation at the Grand Canyon or the Outer Banks, anywhere but Sullivan's Island. And every year her mother had pointed out that they couldn't afford the Grand Canyon or the Outer Banks. "Or even the Inner Banks," her brother Pete would whisper in her ear to make her laugh.

Maggie guessed Pete had liked the island okay, but then, unlike Maggie, Pete had never been a complainer. He had been two and a half years older, but he'd never treated her like a baby the way Ashton did, and Ashton wasn't even one year older.

Maggie hadn't argued with her mother, but she had taken the bus down to her father's office one day near the end of school and had waited in the swivel chair behind his desk until he got out of his afternoon class.

"Hey! Maggie May!" he'd said as he walked through the door. It was his name for her, and it came from some old rock and roll song. He'd downloaded the song for her, but she hadn't been too impressed. Really, she was named Margaret for Aunt Peg.

"Daddy, please let me stay here with you this summer," she'd blurted out and then burst into tears.

"Aw, Maggie, baby," he'd said, pulling her against him and letting her cry against his shirt. "Hush, now, don't."

She had wiped her eyes, angry with herself. She almost never cried. She sat down in the swivel chair at the desk, and her father sat in the other one that was for students.

"You know I'll be teaching this summer. You'd have to sit home by yourself with nothing to do, and you'd hate that."

"Then don't teach. Come to the beach with Mom and me."

Her father had been quiet for a long time. Then he'd said, "I know you don't want to go to the island, honey. But your mother is really looking forward to it. She needs to be with Peg right now, and I guess Peg needs her too. I'd just be in the way." He smoothed back his hair and Maggie saw that it was thinner on top than it had been not long ago. "I know it's hard for you to understand, but your mother and I need some time apart. This thing with Pete has been hard on us. On you too, Mags, I know that. Maybe harder on you than on us."

Maggie hung her head. It had happened on the dull and anticlimactic day after Christmas. Pete had come home from the hospital on Christmas Eve, and he had been scheduled to go back that afternoon. He'd seemed to feel okay Christmas morning, and he'd actually eaten a little of the Christmas dinner. Or maybe he'd been faking it, trying not to spoil the holidays. She had found him. He'd been sleeping a lot, but when he hadn't emerged from his room at noon, her mother had sent her to wake him.

He had been face down in his rumpled bed, and when Maggie had grabbed his shoulder she'd felt both heat and absence. He was burning with fever, and blood had flowed from his mouth and nose, turning the upper third of his sheet maroon. The doctor said his platelet count had dropped to almost nothing, so that his blood couldn't clot. The blood cells that fight infection were too low. They gave him blood transfusions and antibiotics, but he'd lived only a day longer.

Pete had been sick for almost three years and dead for six months, but it still seemed a little unreal to Maggie, like something she had dreamed. Leukemia. Even the word itself seemed remote, fanciful, like some old-fashioned girl's name or some tiny, faraway country. Lavinia, Monrovia, Leukemia.

Oddly enough, here at the beach, Pete's death seemed more true than it had at home. And yet, somehow, he seemed very near, as though he might at any moment step out from behind a dune, or come banging through the back door of the cottage, all excited about some new shell he'd found.

"Let's go and see if Sean and Chris want to play volleyball," Ashton said. Tim or Tom or whoever he was hadn't been at Gorgan's, so Maggie and Ashton had started back down the narrow road that ran behind the first row of beach cottages. Sean and Chris and several other college boys had rented the house three doors down from Aunt Peg's. Ashton actually got off her towel-covered lounge chair when they appeared on the beach with their volleyball net and beer and ran around chasing their bad serves and out-of-bounds shots.

"I saw them all leave a little while ago," Maggie had lied. She had no intention of going to their stupid house. Ashton knew how to joke around the boys, even college boys, teasing them and laughing at their jokes and pretending to be mad at them, even when she wasn't. The one named Sean kept asking Ashton if she was really fourteen, which was how old she had told them she was. "Are you sure you're not sixteen, or maybe eighteen?" he'd say, and the others would laugh. Maggie wasn't sure, but she thought they might be making fun of Ashton, or something worse. She didn't like the funny feeling that gave her. She was used to thinking of boys as part of the scenery, like squirrels or pine trees.

"Well, let's see if our moms will take us into town then. Or to the mall."

"I don't want to go to the mall." Maggie banged through the screen door and walked past the kitchen table where her mother and Aunt Peg sat. They had mixed a pitcher of sangria before lunch and they'd been sitting there with it ever since. Or maybe this was a new pitcher.

Maggie went into the bedroom she shared with Ashton and sat on the edge of her bed. The cottage had four bedrooms. Maggie hadn't wanted to share, but her mother had insisted. "That's part of the fun, staying up late and talking, telling secrets." She hadn't argued with her mother because there was no point talking to somebody who thought there was any chance that Maggie and Ashton were going to whisper and giggle into the night.

"I'm bored," Ashton announced, trailing into the bedroom after Maggie. She pushed a heap of clothes off her bed and flopped full length on it. Maggie had wanted the bed by the window, but Ashton had claimed it.

"You want to borrow a book?" Maggie had a dozen, including the vampire books that every girl her age was crazy for. Her dad had bought them for her as a surprise, to bring to the beach. She'd read the first one; it was stupid and more a high school romance book than a scary one. The reason the vampires couldn't go out into the sun was because they glittered, not because it killed. Please. She held out the third one in the trilogy to Ashton, who'd never finish it anyway. She had some kind of learning problem and could barely read. Maggie had heard her mom talking to Aunt Peg on the phone about the testing Ashton was having.

"No, thanks.," Ashton had unearthed her laptop from the mess on the floor and was checking her e-mail, which she did about twenty times a day. "Hey, let's pluck our eyebrows."

"Gross." Maggie stood up. "I'm going swimming." She took her old Speedo, so chlorine faded you couldn't tell what color it had been, into the bathroom to change. She went out the side door, hoping to escape, but before she reached the sand, she heard the screen door slam. "Damn, damn, damn," she muttered, not looking back.

"Let's play the truth game," Ashton caught up to Maggie as she crossed the wide, low-tide beach.

"No." Maggie stopped walking. "It's a stupid game."

"It's not!" Ashton pouted. "Besides, it's your game. You made it up."

It was true. Maggie had thought of the game one rainy day the summer before, and until Pete made them stop, it had escalated into verbal guerilla warfare between the two girls.

"You have to tell me something even my best friend wouldn't tell me," Maggie had said. "And then I'll do the same for you. And we can't get mad, or tell on each other, or anything."

"Maggie, that's retarded," Pete had argued. "Let's play Monopoly or Life or something. Or we could play a video game." Ashton had her own Xbox, and Pete loved it. Their dad said video games rot your brain, and he wouldn't buy them one, but he didn't mind if they played Ashton's.

"No, no," Ashton had said. "Let's play Maggie's game." Pete wouldn't play, but he was forced to referee.

"Hey wait, Mags, it has to be true," he'd warned, catching her in a lie.

So, she'd said, "The truth is, Pete will buy me ice cream out of his allowance." Sighing, he had, so that she wouldn't be a liar.

Then Ashton had said, "The truth is, Pete is going to give me the next conch shell he finds instead of giving it to Maggie."

"Are you?" Maggie had demanded. They all knew Maggie desperately wanted a perfect conch for her shell collection. When Pete had said yes, she'd spitefully said, "Okay then. The truth is, Pete's voice cracks every time he talks to Emily Hendrix."

Ashton giggled, but Pete's face turned red, and he'd said, "That's it. You're not playing this rotten game anymore. If you do, I'll tell Mother."

Pete almost never told on her, and Maggie knew she'd made him really mad. "Okay, chill out," she'd told him, already a little sorry for what she'd said. Now, thinking about it, she was more than a little sorry.

"I'll go first." Ashton stopped at the edge of the water. "The truth is: You've got sand all over your butt." She burst into peals of laughter as Maggie brushed at the seat of her bathing suit. She never rinsed it after she swam like she was supposed to.

Maggie plunged into the surf and kept wading until the biggest waves lifted her feet off the ocean's bottom. The water was cold, though, and she gave in and headed back to the beach where Ashton waited. "The truth is," she said, wiping stinging saltwater out of her eyes, "Ashton is a boy's name. That means you're a lesbian."

"I am not! You are!" Ashton's nostrils flared, which from experience Maggie recognized as a danger sign. "But if I was, the truth is, I wouldn't let you be my girlfriend because you're so skinny and ugly."

"The truth is," Maggie headed down the beach, leading Ashton away from the house as a weak sun began to burn away the clouds. "I wouldn't be your girlfriend anyway because you're so fat and ugly." They walked all the way down the beach and back exchanging bits of vitriol.

"The truth is," Ashton hissed behind Maggie's back as she opened the screen door, "your bathing suit is an embarrassment, I heard your mother say so, but you're too stubborn to let her buy you a new one." That was true, but it stung to know her mother had said so.

"The truth is," Maggie shouted over Ashton's blow dryer as they got ready to go out to dinner, "gold nail polish is tacky."

At the restaurant Ashton whispered between bites of shrimp, "The truth is, your dad is a loser. My mom said so."

Maggie whispered back, "The truth is, your mom is a money-grubber. My dad said so."

In the back seat of Aunt Peg's Escalade, Ashton murmured, "The truth is, your mom is ashamed of you because you're so dumb."

They could hardly brush their teeth for talking, spitting venom through bristles and toothpaste foam, until finally, as they lay in their narrow, musty-smelling beds, their mothers' voices just audible from the kitchen, Maggie said into the moonlit darkness, "The truth is, you are the real reason your parents are getting a divorce. Neither of them wants you."

Ashton sat straight up in her bed, the moonlight through the window catching her hair. "That's not true!" She choked back tears. Then she said, "The real truth is, your mom and dad wish you had died instead of Pete. They liked him better than you!"

And because Maggie deeply feared that this was the truth, she sprang up in her own bed, nearly hissing at the other girl, "The truth is, when the moon goes down and it's really dark, Pete will come for you."

"Don't be mean, Maggie." Ashton's voice was thin and shrill. "Take it back. Right now." She dug the rag of a baby blanket she didn't want Maggie to know she had from under her pillow and clutched it to her chest and curled herself around it.

"I can't." Maggie lay back, crossing her arms behind her head. "It's the truth."

"Maggie," Ashton's voice was pleading.

"Hush, Ashton. Just watch the moon set because that's when he'll come for you."

For long minutes they lay still in their beds, watching the almost-round, yellow moon slide down the sky until its edge slipped below the tops of the crepe myrtles. As clouds blew across the pale flat orb, a darkness darker than the absence of light filled the room. It was the darkness of a cave, a grave, the back side of the moon. Ashton began to sob and Maggie rolled over, smiling into her pillow.

The sound of footsteps in the hallway stopped her breath, and Maggie felt the truth behind the shadow of her lies. The tide of Ashton's cries washed over her as the doorknob turned, and she jerked the blanket over her head and listened, waiting. ✳

BEFORE THE CHICKEN'S FRIED

➤ JOHN LANE

- -

Yesterday, when Geraldine went out to feed the dogs, she found the big one dead in the middle of the muddy pen, his head in the water dish. They put the other one, the female, to sleep later in the day. The big one had died of a heart attack, and the small female was so old she would have followed within a month. Of course, Geraldine called to tell me this. Some mornings I'm up early enough to see her feed the dogs and ducks, but not yesterday.

I stand at my kitchen window watching and sometimes give a little wave. How she got attached to the ducks, I'll never know. She says Herbert liked them, and she never doubted buying the feed since he died. Who am I to question? This morning, it's only her and the ducks.

We talk on the phone mostly and don't visit much except over the wire fence in the back. But when she calls, it's all laughs like old women tend toward when they are alone with each other. The laughing is something special to do between cooking and watching the soaps.

But this morning, there won't be any calls. She's down there standing alone in the dog pen, the two brown ducks waddling around her. I can hear the ducks quacking through the fig trees and the window. She's standing there in the white slip she always wears on Sundays this early in the morning.

Yesterday, her son-in-law took the dogs away, one dead, one soon to be. Geraldine told me this, but I knew his truck when I got up. Big tires, chrome everywhere. I didn't know yet what was wrong, but the truck was there, and it had to be something.

He's a big man who wears a cowboy hat, and I'd know him anywhere. He makes his living playing guitar in a rock band, and when he married Geraldine's daughter, Anne Marie, he gave the two dogs to Herbert as a gift, a peace offering of sorts, since Herbert didn't approve. That was ten years ago.

Geraldine always calls him when she needs help with the dogs. She says he was there yesterday, in the pen, putting a leash on the small one. The dogs gave Geraldine an excuse to get the boy to come around. I call him "boy," but he's probably close to forty now. Geraldine would say, "Since Herbert died, if I need something, all I have to do is call, and Truck will come over." That's what she calls him. His name is Morris, but she always calls him Truck.

In an hour my family will be here. I'm listening to the radio, breaking open a can of biscuits for Sunday dinner, watching Geraldine standing down there in the pen. My son and daughter probably will go down and talk to her if she's still out there. My daughter Jennie is different from most young people. She keeps up with the neighbors, both mine and hers. Her kids couldn't care less; they'll stay up here in front of the TV. Tom, my son, is the same as Jennie. They'll both be down there pushing back the fig limbs to talk to Geraldine. They'll talk and talk and talk. Didn't get it from me.

Some Sundays Jennie's husband Melvin comes. Some he doesn't. But he came every Sunday when we had to clear the rats out of Geraldine's dog pen. I stood up here and watched those rats, twenty or thirty of them, come out of the holes in the roots of the fig trees and climb into the pen.

They formed a little rat parade and would take a piece of dry dog food and head back to their holes. I told Tom and Melvin that the rats were different colors and climbed trees, but they thought it was just another of Geraldine's stories. Then they stood where I am standing and watched one Sunday at dinner. They believed.

Brown rats, white rats, black and tan rats like you buy at the dime store, all climbing up on the limbs of that fig tree and heading in a parade into the dog pen. How could they have gotten so big and colorful? After that, Melvin came every Sunday for a month with his .22 and shot at them. He killed twenty and put them in plastic garbage bags and left them for the trash men to pick up on the street.

He had to stop shooting since I live in town. The city gave us peanut butter laced with poison. That did it. Dead rats everywhere. But also dead squirrels, jaybirds, grackles, even one cat from down the street. Tom laughs to this day and says that we should have filed an environmental impact statement with all the death in the neighborhood. The ducks and the dogs survived it all.

For two weeks Geraldine went out with Playtex gloves at night and threw the dead rats from her yard over her side fence into the Cuban's yard. I even saw her throw a few over here, but I'd go out later on in the night and throw them back.

The Cuban called sometime that week and wanted to know, as well as I could make out through his accent, what it was that smelled so bad on his back lot. I can't even understand him in person. He carefully repeated his question though, and I finally understood.

I told him something might have died back there in the weeds, and maybe he should keep his lot cut and he wouldn't have these problems. The next day, he was out there with a long knife cutting the high grass down. He didn't stay long. Geraldine and I laughed over that one for weeks.

If you can't laugh, then what have you got? That's what we always say. Dinner in this house is always one story after another. Nothing can ever ruin that time. If the turkey's tough or the chicken's still bloody around the bone, just laugh about it. The only time I stop laughing is when my family goes separate ways, and Sunday's over until next week.

On Sunday mornings like this one I get sad thinking about dead dogs and rats and how the day is really over long before the chicken's even fried. Some days I think about that, and some days I feel better. I get this feeling that if I just started moving to some old song I used to know, that my body would move, float through the house like it was riding on a cloud, and I wouldn't think about all those dead things.

I haven't danced in years. Not since I went out with the furniture salesman for a time. He used to take me out to the Hilltop Diner. That was twenty years ago. We danced and drank beer. One night there was a full moon, and he had a convertible, so later in the night we drove to the top of a hill out near Boiling Springs. He stopped the car. I'll have to admit, I was a little afraid, though I was a widow woman. I also had that tingle of excitement. There I was, middle aged and out parking. He turned my face from side to side about ten times, not speaking. I didn't say a word either.

Finally I asked him, "What in God's word are you doing, Jennings?" He smiled and said, "I just wanted to remember what your face looked like in this moonlight."

I wish things would have stopped right there with us stalled in that moonlight in the middle of such a night. But I soon found out he was married, and his wife was dying of cancer. Then, after all this time of him coming around, I find out that he has been buying some other woman a trailer home across town. I told him that there just wasn't enough moonlight for all that. The family laughs about all that now, just like everything else.

Why, look down there. There goes Geraldine. She's finally headed inside. Listen to those ducks. She'll call if she's feeling better. Maybe some Sunday I'll have her up here to eat chicken with the family. Maybe I'll even buy some duck and roast it. She'd get a kick out of that. We're always finding something to dig a laugh from.

The kids might even stop watching TV if Geraldine came up. Or maybe the two of us can just take off one Sunday and go to the Piccadilly Cafeteria out at Westgate and leave the family to fix for itself. We could get some steamship round of beef, mashed potatoes, green beans, salad bar, and sweet tea. I'll call her if she doesn't call first. I'll even ask her if she's heard from the Cuban. That's always good for a laugh or two.

The grease is finally hot, and the chicken's ready to go in. I watch the fat sizzle as each piece starts to cook. Geraldine says duck meat is fat and dark. I turn each leg, thigh, breast, and back. My fingerprints leave a faint stain on the countertop as I put down the fork, turn and look out the window one more time. I always wonder if I've cooked too much.

I also wonder what Geraldine had to eat today. She likes to broil liver wrapped in bacon, held together with toothpicks. Maybe she'll call and tell me. The phone could ring anytime. We play a game with each other, calling at odd times with stories. Geraldine says it's the closest thing to magic that life can offer. ✴

WHERE IS WILLIAM NOW?

> JEREMY L. C. JONES

Meredith, who was eight, kept the bullet slug in a black sock. She slept with it under her pillow. When her daddy got back from the war, he'd make a hole in the slug, so she could wear it as a necklace. For now, it was tucked safely in her pocket.

Meredith strained to see over the truck's dashboard—the barn doors of the feed and machine store, the brick train depot with the red, white, and blue awning, people she knew by name, and others she knew by the dresses and jackets they wore.

Meredith's mother smiled, briefly softening the tight lines of her face. They reached the turn-off for their house. A flag drooped from the porch.

C. Allen leapt to the yard. He was ten, older than Meredith, and stayed home to watch Baby Bessie when Meredith and their mother went to the grocery.

"You got a letter, Ma," he said. "A letter."

Their mother hefted the brown sacks from the payload of the truck and handed them to C. Allen. He ran toward the kitchen, his feet loud on the porch planks. His mother moved slowly toward the mailbox. A corner of the letter showed over the top.

Meredith looked through the rust-flecked hole the bullet had made in door of the truck. This is where it went in, just three years ago, whizzing just above her daddy's shoulders, behind his head, ricocheting inside the truck before it plopped into his lap. Her daddy had come home, trembling but grinning while he told the story to Meredith's mother. Meredith had touched the slug in his palm. It had almost killed her daddy, and she loved her daddy.

He had laughed when he told the story: "I felt it buzzing by my head and I couldn't do a thing."

"Bill, you'll scare the children," Meredith's mother had said.

"I just sat there frozen." He had patted Meredith on the head. "A hunter saw me moving and took a shot."

"Bill, the children."

He'd seemed so alive telling the story.

Twice, since Meredith's father had left for the Philippines, she had seen him in the dim light of the kitchen, skinning apples for her mother's Sunday pie. He never looked up from his work, and she never managed to speak to him.

Seeing her father's ghost only made it worse for her, only reminded her that men died in war and were shipped home in unpainted coffins on trains.

Meredith used rainwater to prime the pump, then filled her red wagon with the cold groundwater. The sun was high and bright above the trees.

She left the wagon in the shade of the trees and scooted on her bottom down the bank to the creek. Meredith sat still until she heard a faint whisper and smelled the crispness of the clear flow. She dipped a smooth gray pebble into the creek and it turned a pale brown. In her mouth, it tasted faintly of salt. The small stone clicked against her teeth as she moved it around with her tongue. Saliva filled her mouth quickly. She spat the pebble into a still pool.

Ripples flexed the smooth surface, settled, and her saliva floated on the surface. She waited. The pebble was lost in the creek bed below. Minnows swarmed to feed on her spit. Deftly, she scooped a Mason jar into the water. The brown-flecked minnows swirled in a haze of sediment in the jar.

Meredith climbed with the half-full jar up to her wagon. Using her cupped palm, she slapped some of the water from the wagon to make room before emptying in the minnows. She did this three more times until the wagon schooled with minnows.

Meredith found the perfect rock, flat on one side, then washed it in the creek and, using both hands, lugged it up to the wagon. She spat in one end of the wagon to distract the minnows so she could position the rock. The rough side rested above the water. Using jars full of dirt, she fashioned a beach of sorts. She plucked a few dandelions and sprigs of grass to landscape the packed dirt. Once she had the wagon set up perfectly, she washed out the jar and went hunting for the orange newts that hid along the creek.

Crouching in the shrubs on the far bank, she thought of when her father told her that her pet newt died, because "wild things weren't meant to live in jars." Her back ached and her thighs burned. Finally, a newt startled from a slick sapling branch. It scurried to the water, leapt in, and paddled frantically.

The current pushed the newt toward the other side of the creek. Meredith straddled a narrow spot in the creek and waited. Water soaked her canvas shoes. The newt was cool between her fingers, ticklish and firm against her cupped palms. She carried it to the wagon and placed it on the stone, the highest part of which had dried in the sun. Stunned, the newt breathed deeply with its whole body. A dead minnow lay on the dirt. The shifting sun warmed Meredith's face.

Meredith knew the newt would not stay long in her perfect world, but the hard part of making the world was done and she could always catch another newt.

Today was train day. Soldiers would be coming in soon, and the whole town would turn out. Meredith slouched in the chair across the table from her mother, who was reading the letter.

"Sit up," her mother said. "You'll get a hump-back."

"What's it say?"

Her mother shuffled the pages. Her father had pressed hard with a pencil; the letters ghosted through the thin paper. Meredith couldn't make out any of the words. Thick black lines from the censors struck out place names and whole lines at a time.

"Well?" she said.

"Hush." Her mother's lips moved as she read. Her shoulders lifted. "He says everything is fine with him, not to worry. And he sends his love to you children."

Meredith blew at her bangs. She slid further down in her chair, pressing the small lump in her pocket and wondering, *what did the letter really say?*

Nobody ever questioned it. Meredith's father had placed the slug on the table and stared at it, shaking his head. Meredith wanted it, so she took it. No one ever asked her what she wanted it for. Her father just stared at the empty space where it had been. For Meredith to take the bullet that had almost killed her daddy was the most natural thing in the world. She pulled a sock from the clothesline, dropped the slug inside, and tried her hardest to go about her life without thinking the most frightening of thoughts.

She waited now in the truck. Her hair was washed and combed straight. A light purple ribbon that matched her flower-print dress held the hair off her neck. A wisp of hair tickled her cheek. She counted to ten and, unable to bear it any longer, blew. She did it again and again. A small part of her wished the hair would flutter away. Another part of her wanted the hair to sting when it touched her skin. It fell back gently against her face every time.

C. Allen ran up the driveway. Meredith opened the truck door and leaned out. "Ma is mad at you," she said. "Where have you been?"

C. Allen dug into his pockets and sunlight flashed off a wad of foil gum and cigarette wrappers. "Collecting tin."

"You're still late," Meredith said.

C. Allen retrieved a fallen gum wrapper, licked his finger, and snapped Meredith a full salute.

"There you are," their mother said from the porch. She used the guide rail for balance as she came down the steps. Baby Bessie's bassinet hung from the crook of her other arm. After having Baby Bessie, one of her legs was permanently weak. Meredith suspected her mother was making it all up to get attention. Something about her mother limping while her father was at war seemed selfish.

"What did the letter say?" C. Allen asked. "Has dad killed any Japs yet?"

"Never you mind." Once in the truck's cab, their mother said, "We're going to be late."

Their mother handed the bassinet over Meredith to C. Allen. He placed it on the floorboard between his feet.

Baby Bessie smelled of sour milk and talcum powder. Meredith crossed her arms and looked straight ahead. On the way into town, C. Allen tickled Baby Bessie's chin. The giggling was broken and wet, but filled with delight. The truck jostled over a crack in the road. Baby Bessie's face reddened and she cried. C. Allen soothed her by petting the soft, white hair on her head.

Meredith itched all over. She squeezed her chest tighter. Years ago, when she caught her knee on a rusted nail, her father had said, "The best thing about hurt is that it gets better."

And he was right: cuts, scrapes, and bruises always went away. Her daddy truly understood her, understood it all. Everything.

An itch on her back got worse, not better. She pressed against the seat, squirmed. Hot pieces of light scattered around inside the cab, bounced off faces, off her mother's knee, bare where her dress had risen up, off C. Allen's farmer's dungarees that embarrassed their mother but that he loved, off the hair of his forearm, off the bristled hair on his neck as he leaned forward to comfort Baby Bessie, off Meredith's own lap.

Meredith said, "I don't see why we have to go to the depot every time soldiers come home."

Baby Bessie writhed for C. Allen's attention. Their mother parked the truck a few blocks up from the red, white, and blue awning. The truck's engine sputtered. C. Allen opened the door and picked up the bassinet. The slug was warm in her pocket, and she pictured it smacking into her father's head like a rock thrown into the muddy bank of the creek after a rainstorm. She had dreamed about it many times. But the picture in her head now was as bland and empty as strangers in the newspaper.

"We are doing our part." Her mother spoke slowly. She slid the letter from the pocket of her skirt and thumbed the stamps. "We have to show our support."

"Daddy isn't coming home," Meredith said. It sprang from her mouth with a life of its own. She felt mean. "Not today," she blurted. "Not ever."

Her mother grabbed Meredith's arm. "Don't. Don't you ever say that, Meredith." Her mother's hand tightened. Meredith's whole body shook. "Never again. Do you hear?"

Meredith wanted to scream: he loves me more, he loves me more. He's alive, alive and well and coming home on the very next train. Coming home to *me*, coming home to pick me up in his arms and spin me around and kiss me and love me. Love *me*.

But she didn't. She couldn't. She struggled to get away from her mother's grip.

"Answer me," her mother said. "Answer me, young lady."

Meredith pulled loose, slid across the seat. She pushed past C. Allen and Baby Bessie and ran toward the growing crowd at the depot.

"He loves me, he loves me." She breathed deeply and rapidly. "He loves me, he loves me."

Meredith hid behind the ticket office while the train came in. The ground rumbled and the bricks hummed with the power of the great machine. A cinder landed by her foot, and she kicked it off the raised landing. When the brake keening stopped, she took the sock from her pocket and wrapped it around her hand. She counted to ten, picturing the numbers her daddy had written inside the chalk hopscotch squares on the sidewalk. It was the day he told her that he would be going to war—that he had volunteered and *wanted* to go. He was too old to get letters from the government like the other fathers. But he *had* to go, and they would let him.

"No," she had said. "No."

But he still went to war.

Meredith pushed her way into the legs and arms, Sunday dresses and dark suits, soldiers in tan uniforms and sailors in white. She knew faces or names, families or farms or towns, curled hair or slicked hair or blond or red or ribboned hair. Here were parts of all the people she knew in the world—all but one. People cheered and cried and hooted and sang and giggled. They sobbed and called out over the music of a hidden radio.

Meredith tried to look on a whole face or hear a complete word, and as she was shoved further out from under the awning's shade, she looked up at a familiar-looking jaw, a nose, the outline of a mouth. Then the backlit profile disappeared and left only the glare of the sun. The crowd shifted off toward the street and the parked cars and the homes, where tonight their parties would be held to celebrate homecoming.

It all pressed at her chest and twisted her face until she felt the hard knot in the toe of the sock. Surely, she thought, there were dozens like it now, dozens of bullets that had not killed her father.

Meredith dangled her legs over the edge of the landing. To her right, the wheels and cranks of the train were greased and hot. A soldier, sitting alone inside a railcar, smiled at her from the window of the train. She waved to him. Small clusters of people chatted and laughed.

A thin, dark-haired boy approached her from up the street. From Meredith's elevated position, he looked small and sad. His wool pants were folded up at the ends. He wore heavy, black shoes. One sole was higher than the other, and he swayed when he walked. Meredith had never seen him before. She hid the sock and slug.

The boy stopped in front of her. His face was damp and pale. He breathed through his mouth. He said, "Why are you so sad?"

Meredith shrugged.

"I'm sad, too," he said. His words were stiff and crisp, as though he'd lived in the city where people don't know each other. He climbed the steps to the landing. Meredith squinted up at him. He moved slightly to block the sun, and his shadow draped over her.

"Do you mind if I join you?"

"Okay." She wasn't sure whether he was pretending to be snooty. His presence next to her was comfortable.

"My name is Edward."

"Mine's Meredith."

They watched their shoes swing back and forth over the edge of the landing.

"What was that you put in your pocket?" Edward asked after a while.

"Being nosy is rude," Meredith said, though she was already unrolling the sock. "Do you really want to know?"

He nodded.

Meredith let the slug slide into her palm.

"This went so close to my daddy's head he could hear it."

Edward picked at his lips and stared curiously at the dimpled lead.

"May I touch it?"

A small piece of fear dried in her throat.

Very gently, he rubbed the rounded end of the slug with a fingertip, as if he were petting a delicate animal. Like a newt's head, Meredith thought. An unfamiliar thrill spread throughout her stomach and chest.

"It's beautiful," he said. "Truly beautiful."

He sounded much older. She wanted to hug him.

"Thank you," she said, closing her fingers around the slug.

"My father died," Edward said. "He was killed by a bomb in France. My mother got a letter."

Meredith breathed deeply, her pulse thumping in her ears.

"It's all right," Edward said. "I almost didn't know him at all. I was young when he left. My mother and I lived in the city for a while, but she lost her job. We're staying with my Nonny and Grandpa now."

Meredith covered her mouth with her free hand. The world was clear and simple to him. She wished her mother had lost her job and that she could sit at the train depot and say her father had died, without crying, without the grass ripping from the earth, without the sky tearing open.

Then she did begin to cry, and Edward patted her shoulder. She wanted this strange boy to tell her that she would be okay, but more than that she wanted a promise from him, a promise that her father wouldn't die.

"That really is a wonderful bullet," he said. "Could I see it again?"

She nodded. "It keeps him from dying, you know."

He took it from her extended hand and held it up close to his eyes. He rolled it between his thumb and forefinger.

"Keep it for me," Meredith said. "Hold onto it for me." She hopped down from the landing and rushed toward her mother, who was talking to other wives whose husbands were off to war.

"Thank you," Edward called.

Meredith turned and waved. Her steps felt light and springy. She almost stumbled.

As Meredith approached, her mother smiled. Meredith climbed in the truck. A woman wearing a dress the same shade as the ribbon in Meredith's hair leaned over Baby Bessie and said, "So, where is William now?"

"Somewhere in the South Pacific," Meredith's mother said. "On a ship between Australia and the Philippines."

Meredith pictured her daddy high up on the top of a big boat, waving to her, calling out to her. The sky was clear and blue. No bullets were whizzing by. His mouth moved. But Meredith could not hear what he was saying. *

I REMEMBER YOU

> WENDY KING

Big Jack waits for Macy, waits for her with a dogged intensity that rivals his devotion to drink, waits for her arrival every evening at the bar, just the same as the evening before, in anticipation of the moment when she will pause before him, the smell of perfume rising from her heat-dampened skin, and pour out, not his first drink of the day, but the first of the day from her hands, as sweet to him as the powdery perfection of her scent. Big Jack watches her movements behind the bar, practiced and confident. Big Jack has learned a lot about Macy just by watching her this way. He knows that she enjoys being a bartender and likes her partner behind the bar, an extremely good-looking boy she calls Mac, who lives in one of those antebellum houses near the Battery. Mac says he works to meet people, not for the money. They both meet many people, sometimes laughing at the end of the evening over which of them is supposed to be the recipient of a particular note they have dug out of the tip jar. The notes are written on cocktail napkins and are not often original.

"Take a good look at the floor, because you'll be looking at the ceiling the rest of the night." "I want to ride you like a Harley over a bumpy road." "I don't want to sleep with you or anything, but I just have to tell you, you are the most beautiful woman I've ever seen."

Phone numbers. Hotel addresses. Street corners and times.

Macy does not pursue these notes, even if she knows which face to connect to the writing. She is a good bartender. She has an inviting smile and warm eyes, shows no preference, is universally charming.

As her estranged husband once said of her, she's built for speed. She can also make drinks and open twist cap beer bottles with her bare hands. She can talk anything with anybody and can set up conversations among the most disparate of customers. Big Jack says she is like a geisha, only with a hick accent.

She pours out another slug for him, lets the bourbon slosh out of his shot glass as she pops it down on the counter and sing-songs, "Back in Nagasaki where the fellows chew tobaccy and the women wicki-wacki woo." Her voice is not good but her memory is magnificent, and when Big Jack is drunk enough he will goad her into crooning some tune that even he can't remember all the words to anymore. He wants to know where she learned all these songs but he's afraid he might shatter the illusion he has built up around her, the illusion that Macy is his own personal angel, patting his shaking yellow-tipped fingers with her cold hands, providing him with the necessary amount of booze each evening, and seeing that he doesn't bump his head on the cab doorframe when she sends him home at night.

Big Jack drinks big, the way he has he lived, and the bar lets him sit there night after night because he is an institution now, the one who wrote them out of their obscurity, put their locales on the big screen, drags in the tourism dollars like they never would have believed. He sits there like a refugee from a black-and-white film, an age of daring young war heroes, splendid with invisible medals gleaming on his broken-down chest.

He loves talking to Macy, telling her his stories again and again, and every time Macy listens as if for the first time, obliges him with songs, shares her own life story, what bits of it she chooses. She never tells him he's had too many. He wishes he had words left. He wishes he hadn't wasted them all on other women, other stories. If he could, he would make Macy his last great story, paint her in the black cocktail dress that is her bartending uniform and the large fake pearl earrings and the hair that she wears in curls in the front and back, like a USO girl of World War II. He hopes she wears it like that to please him, never thinking that it is an affectation and a costume, like the vintage dress and cheap pearls. He thinks of asking her to marry him, though he is old enough to be her grandfather, and imagines her as the last wife in a string that predates her own birth by decades. He has no reason to believe that she would accept. He can't see an ounce of gold-digger in her. The many offers she refuses have shown him that plainly. She could make far more than she does by taking off that black dress in the hotel rooms that wait all over the city for her. She is without a doubt a fine creation, and he wishes he had made her. Such a character would last beyond him, in a way that he is not sure his other work will. He wonders sometimes if they will rename the bar for him after he is dead. He wonders if he should ask it as a favor, and see to it that they call it after Macy's name for him, Big Jack Cadillac. The Big Jack Cadillac Room. It is far too classy a bar for that to ever happen, though, and he knows that if it were dedicated to his memory, the more familiar name will be cut into the polished brass plaque. If only he had the words left, he would write this story, put it into a form the world would be willing to recognize. In his own fading away, he wants to be certain that Macy will always be admired, always be beautiful, her remarkable talents documented.

Back in the winter, the first evening he came in and found Macy there behind the bar, she had been wearing a wedding ring, which he has noticed missing from her finger these last few weeks. He has heard her tell Mac that her divorce will be made final any day and he is determined then to present himself as a likely candidate. He doesn't know the reason why Macy wanted one, although he can certainly imagine enough scenarios, many of which he has experienced firsthand.

His first wife, a healthy blonde with great legs who spent all the allotment checks sent to her so that by war's end they hadn't a penny to start out on, had left him for a man with a more promising future. Jack is sure that somewhere there sits a fat, coarse woman still bemoaning her ill-fortune to some long-suffering soul who wishes too that she had never left her first husband.

The second and third wives, both pretty and well-bred, whom he had deceived again and again until neither one would even look him in the face, refused his money and finally his name. The fourth wife, Martha, also pretty and well-bred, fantastically fine-boned, he had loved and been faithful to until the very end. She was not very old when she died, though he was already then an old man, and in the ten years since her death he has been drinking more heavily than ever before in his life, though his drinking was always a problem, with wives one through four. Macy, though, he is sure, would never nag, just like Martha, who treated him with the sure hand and wit of a Nora Charles. She was a classy woman whose sense of humor never failed her, not even at the end.

He had never lived up to her image of him. Always he was a blundering redneck, never a debonair, mustachioed leading man, and though she never alluded to his awkwardness, she plainly knew they were an odd match. Macy, on the other hand, is his perfect match, the woman who should have served him doughnuts and coffee at the USO bar and married him in a rush at the magistrate's office, saved her pennies, planted a Victory garden on the windowsill, waited for his return from the Pacific theatre anxiously, and thrown her arms around him with joy when he came home. She would not be embarrassed at being found in denims, dusting the small apartment that would never seem too small, not even after a baby and a dog, she would have been at home in a hunting cabin or a luxury liner, might have stopped his drinking and made him a better writer, one who wouldn't have to worry, as he does, that every word he's put down on paper will evaporate when he is gone, that the force of his personality is all that keeps the world's interest, making him a landmark on a bar stool.

Macy, meanwhile, unaware of his thoughts, offers another drink and pats his hand, smiles her extraordinary smile, and moves on to another customer, one who chats her up challengingly. She plays her game, flirts and flatters, and Jack knows that they will laugh later over the scribbled come-on of the cocktail napkin and the large tip folded up inside, as if Macy is that cheap, as if Macy doesn't see through them. She is a tough, career-minded girl, one with a past, never a leading lady, a woman whose happy ending waits in the wings, after the credits roll. He can't change Macy's fate, the role she was made to play, the legs crafted to wear stockings with seams, her lips red with pasty drugstore lipstick, but he can imagine her future without him, growing a few years older, falling for the wrong man again because the right one never seems to come along. He sees her working hard, maybe owning her own place, closing up at night, tucking the receipts in the drawer, turning off the lights, her high-heeled footsteps echoing down a city street, farther and farther away from him.

Macy watches Big Jack's head sink down onto the bar and picks up the phone, dials the cab company, jokes with the dispatcher with whom she is on a first-name basis, and starts closing up for the night. The tip jar is full, and she and Mac divvy up the contents. They wash the last glasses, all the customers but Big Jack having left already, put a rope up at the door, the liquor laws in effect now, and they wait for the beep of a taxicab's horn. Macy and Mac wrangle Big Jack's lumbrous form out the door and into the cab, Macy putting her hand on the top of his greasy grey head and easing him into the backseat. When she reaches in to fasten the seat belt he wakes up a little, grabs her waist and asks her to marry him. "Sure, Big Jack, any time you say." She pats his hands, removes them from her waist, and closes the cab door. Big Jack looks out at her with a face full of love, a moony dream face, a drunken old-man face transfigured by his passion for the hand that pours the bourbon. Macy asks Mac if he thinks Big Jack will be upset that she is leaving, that tonight was her last night. Mac says her ass is nice, but not that nice, and that Big Jack will slobber over the next pretty face that holds his bottle for him. Macy punches his arm, laughing. Standing at the door to the bar, looking out on the deserted street, she has the feeling of being left behind by the last train out of the station and hears, somewhere, passing through the city, a train blowing its whistle, the echo of it like the memory of something she used to know, a crowded station suddenly empty except for the smell of cheap perfume, her face smudged with tears, looking down the tracks after a military train, bits of red, white, and blue bunting trailing along behind it in a patriotic confetti that settles like paper snow at her feet. The feeling passes, the image fading along with the train whistle into the early morning, and she steps into the bar, closing the door firmly behind her. ✳

HOT NOW

> MOLLY KNIGHT

Do you think it's weird that I never laugh when I'm alone? Like when I used to watch funny movies by myself on Saturday afternoons. Not that it matters now, I guess. I like college though, really I do. It's just that you're not alone very much. That's all I mean. Like the other day a girl on my hall walked in on me in the shower. Maybe I'm wrong to say this, but I think she meant to do it. Really, she had to have seen my shower shoes, they're bright pink, and besides, she's just the type. But anyway, I felt so *naked* standing there—I mean I was, but—I guess I wouldn't have minded so much except nobody's ever seen me naked before. Not even my momma, after she stopped giving me baths. I always thought the first one to see me that way would be a boy. Or a man, I guess. Maybe I shouldn't be thinking about that at all, though, right? Especially in the shower.

In any case, I'm not much to look at. All those college boys I thought would swarm me haven't given me the time of day since I got to Furman. My grandma had thirteen children, and I seem to have inherited her good birthing hips. And you know that thing about the Freshman Fifteen? They're not kidding. I'm turning into such a hog, I blend in with the livestock when I come home to Blacksburg on the weekends. Like last Thursday night I went to Krispy Kreme instead of Praise and Worship. This girl Erica from across the hall said she didn't really feel like going; I even suggested making a doughnut run.

So there we were in my Land Rover at eleven o'clock at night, pulling into Krispy Kreme. I felt so guilty on the way. We talked about Praise

137

and Worship the whole way there—how these two Furman boys started it as a little Christian music group that played in their dorm's common room, and how now the crowds are so big they keep getting kicked out of the meeting places. It's kind of Biblical, if you think about it. Like Mary and Joseph getting sent away from the inns. There's nothing like this big holy noise blasting out of those amps and speakers, with people shoulder to shoulder all around—but have you ever noticed how *safe* Krispy Kreme feels? I used to sit in the car and watch the lights flash while my daddy went in to get us something. Red-and-green, red-and-green. My brother always says it looks like a whorehouse. I try not to listen to him.

The HOT NOW sign wasn't on when Erica and I got there, so hardly anybody was in there except us and the lady behind the counter. She was young, I guess, black, and she had a hairnet on. Black people always seem to look at me mean. I suppose it could just be me, and anyway the Lord said not to judge, but I can't help being nervous sometimes.

I needed a minute to pick out which kind I wanted, so Erica went ahead and ordered hers and everyone else's along with a dozen plain. The plain ones were to put in the kitchen for everybody to share—I thought that was sweet of her. She's like that. Something about her face—her mouth or her long eyelashes, maybe—makes her look a little gloomy, but really, she's always making everybody happy, so she's got to be OK, too. I don't know her very well.

I ordered a plain after all, since I couldn't make up my mind about the fancy ones, and a nice big coffee. I think you're always sleepy in college—it's not really true that everyone's up all night studying, though. They party. Or so I hear, I mean, I've never actually been to one of the parties, but people tell me about them. And sometimes I can hear them while I'm in bed, on the floor above or below me. Never on mine, though, because I'm on the substance-free hall.

It took some getting used to, all the noise; in Gaffney at night the quiet gets in your ears, and you might as well be the only person in the world. I don't know which is scarier, the quiet or the noise.

That's when I noticed the lady at the other table. All by herself, no food, her purse on the table in front of her. Just sitting there with both hands in her lap. She must've been sixty, but I couldn't really tell, because her hair was still brown, but she had on one of those mock turtlenecks that only grandmas wear. Then all of a sudden her eyes came into focus like, and she smiled at me.

"How's your doughnut?" she said.

I just grinned and shrugged at her, you know, being polite. I've never liked talking to strangers, but my momma taught me to always act like I do, because it's nice and people expect it. "Great," I said, after I'd swallowed, and then I asked, "Why don't you have one?" I guess maybe Momma'd say that was rude, but I couldn't think of anything else.

The lady didn't seem to think it was. She said, "I'm here to try and get a job working back there, packing up doughnuts, maybe. Don't have nothing else better to do. I live over to other side of town, but that's OK. I used to live in California. It's awful nice over there, and I had a two-story house and it wasn't too far back from the beach. I bet you like the beach, since you can wear a pretty bikini. But come on over here and talk to me," and she patted the seat next to her.

Well, I just didn't know what to do. After listening to her a while, I'd figured out that this weird sound in her voice, kind of like a foreign accent, meant she was retarded. She looked like she could've been pretty when she was young, though; I thought it was a real shame, you know. So I took my coffee and went and sat down next to her. I swear I don't think I took a breath for five minutes. Really I didn't have to say much at all., She barely took a breath herself, she talked so much. About California, Greenville, Charleston. Her grown daughter lived in Charleston, at least that's what I think she said. Oh, and her grandbaby, and the little clothes she'd bought it, and the bookcase full of books she'd given it that used to be her daughter's. All of this she talked about to some strange girl in the Krispy Kreme.

But all of a sudden, while I was sitting there, I got to feeling really good, like you do at Praise and Worship or driving in a go-cart race at International Pavilion. I guess it was because I was being there, you know, for somebody, and nothing else about me mattered just then. I wonder if that's how mothers feel.

Meanwhile Erica had bought herself a shirt and was back at our table, giving me a funny look, like the one my brother would have given me. But I just couldn't shake that feeling, so I just smiled big like they taught us at deb club and waved her over to us. She ate up the last of her doughnut, sat down beside me, looked at the lady sideways through her thick eyelashes, and introduced herself. She was nervous like I'd been, but I figured she'd realize what a wonderful opportunity it all was, maybe by the time we got back to the car.

I took a deep breath and proposed a prayer for the first time in my life. "Why don't we have a prayer for our new friend?" I said. Erica grinned a little with one side of her mouth. I think she saw. The woman uncrossed her arms from over her big grandma chest, and we held hands around the table. Erica's was a little sticky from the donuts, but the woman's was warm and dry, like it'd just been lying around open in the sun. Like prayer hands ought to be.

"Dear Lord," I said, "we thank you for our Savior Jesus Christ, for giving up your only son so we could be saved, dear Lord, and we ask that you ... wait." Everybody looked up. "I'm sorry, what's your name, ma'am?" I couldn't believe I hadn't thought of that beforehand.

"Anita," she said.

I took another deep breath, bowed my head. I feel like maybe Erica didn't bow her head, but you know, to each his own. "Dear Lord," I said, "we thank you for our Savior Jesus Christ, for giving up your only son so we could be saved, dear Lord, and please forgive me for interrupting the prayer before. We ask that you please watch over Anita tonight, dear Lord, and help her get this job, and keep her safe on her way home. And please, dear Lord, watch over Erica and me on the way back, too. Thank you, dear Lord, in Jesus' name we pray, A-men."

When she finally opened her eyes, Anita just smiled and smiled at me with this blank look on her face, without saying thanks or anything, and all of a sudden I felt like getting on back to the car. So I got up and said, "Bye, Anita, good luck," and Erica got up too, and we went outside.

After the door jingled shut, I stopped in the parking lot for a minute and looked around. It felt dark and still and quiet like my yard used to, and the world seemed waiting for me to do something. I don't know what I was expecting, though, I guess. I just went on and cranked up the car and headed for the campus with Erica beside me. After a minute I said, "She was sweet, wasn't she?"

"Yeah." She was picking at the edge of the doughnut box.

"I'm glad we could pray for her."

By that time all my big excited feelings were just about gone. When I got back to my dorm room, I tried to call my momma and tell her about it, but she was already asleep and my brother answered, so I told him instead. Now he wants to go back there next week and see if she got the job. I told him "Love you, g'night," like I hadn't heard him, and went back out to catch the end of Praise and Worship. It runs into the wee hours, sometimes. ✳

YOU'VE CHANGED

➤ CAROL J. ISLER

I kicked off my boots, collapsed in the middle of the swing, stretched my arms across the backrest, and tilted my head back to stare at the beaded lapboards on the porch ceiling of the old home place near Swannanoa. The whitewashed boards appeared pink in the glow of the sun, just setting over the ridge behind the house. Teetering the swing at its balance point, I pushed myself back and forth with my toes. More than halfway toward my goal, I was feeling very satisfied. Nobody else would have these mountain plants in their collections.

Footsteps crunched in the fallen white oak leaves around the corner of the house. I stilled and was quiet. My cousin walked straight out to his Bondoed and primer gray pickup truck parked in front of the pasture gate. I turned sideways in the swing and propped my bare feet in it, watching him.

Eddie carried a pruning saw, ax, and long-handled limb loppers. The old '59 Chevy's door squeaked when opened, and he dropped the tools behind the seat with a metallic clang. After rubbing his hands down the legs of his overalls, he slammed the door and leaned on the front fender, staring out over the pasture toward the sunset.

I fumbled for the pack of cigarettes in the front pocket of my overalls and chuckled at the thought of our similar outfits. I remembered the first time I donned overalls, on an environmental studies field trip; I was the laughingstock of the class. Being a practical girl who wanted to be comfortable when she worked, I didn't let it bother me. Before the end of the spring semester, Oshkosh overalls, white tank tops, Vasque hiking boots, and wide-brimmed straw hats had become the rage in Dr. Powell's ecology class at Converse.

With the mentholed Marlboro between my lips, I clicked my lighter. It didn't work. I shook it. Click. Nothing. "Crap." I threw the lighter down on the porch boards.

Now at the foot of the porch steps, Eddie watched me. "How long you been doing that, Katie?" he asked, crossing his arms and frowning.

"I've been sitting here about ten minutes, I guess."

"No. I mean smoking." Eddie flung out his arms. "How long you been smoking?"

"When I took calculus last year I started. Why? No big deal. Everybody up here smokes, dips, or chews," I said in defense.

"I don't," he almost whispered. He propped a foot high on the steps and leaned over his thigh with his arms crossed, glaring at me.

I rolled my eyes and turned around straight in the swing, patting the empty seat beside me. "Want to show you what I found." I pulled open one of my sacks, dumped its contents on the floor in front of me, grabbed a plastic bag, and sniffed it. "This is it, Eddie. I can't find this in Spartanburg, Sweet Scented Joe Pye Weed." I took out a leaf, crushed it between my fingers and sniffed again. "It's like vanilla. Come here and smell it."

"I know how it smells."

"Eddie! What's wrong with you?" I patted the seat again. "Come sit by me."

He shook his head. "Them bad storms last week left a mess up there." He gestured toward the ridge. "Been clearing the road. I stink bad."

"Me, too," I sniffed my armpit and grimaced. "Pew! My boots are pretty bad, too. You wanna smell?" As I offered a boot, I laughed, but Eddie didn't. He just wiped the sweat from his face with his sleeve, clearing a clean spot from brow to chin.

"You been working alone?" I asked. "I just wondered 'cause you told me not to ever go up there by my own self. So I stayed down here all day collecting plants from the fence rows and the edge of the woods."

"Uncle Sonny's helping me."

"Oh." I nodded and sighed. "Yeah, I heard chopping and a chainsaw, but I couldn't tell where it was coming from." The sounds echoed all over the cove.

I pulled the rubber band from the end of my braid and shook it loose, combing my fingers through my hair to unravel it. With both hands, I raked up and out through my hair, now wavy from the braid, letting the air reach my sweaty scalp. I stretched, inhaling the mountain deeply and collapsed back into the swing.

Lolling my head against the backrest of the swing, I smiled at Eddie. "Awful hot for early October, ain't it?" I said, stalling. I didn't want him to walk away. I wanted to talk to my cousin, tell him about how his old friend, John, was doing since he came to Spartanburg to school.

"Yup."

We just stared at each other for a while, and then he walked away.

"Eddie!"

He turned back around. "What?"

"Why don't you talk to me anymore? You've been avoiding me for months." I picked little pieces of stems and leaves off my clothes and flicked them over the porch railing. "Every time I come up here you do this. And you haven't come to our place in over a year."

He shrugged. "Things changed."

"Like what?" I asked.

"You're getting too educated down at that there college to fool with me. It ain't the same. You ain't the same," Eddie walked back to the steps.

"No." I shook my finger at him. "You're not the same. I'm still me."

"Sometimes I think you're trying to make me feel stupid," Eddie said.

"What? I would never do that on purpose, Eddie." I was shocked that he felt that way. "It's just that sometimes I get excited about the stuff I'm learning, and I want to share it with you."

"Share it?" He came up one step closer.

"Yeah, just like when we were little. You would get so excited about something on this mountain and you had to share it with me. The bear cave, the old burial ground, and arrowheads," I whipped my wrist in the air. "Fly fishing for trout, and male snakes," I said and laughed.

He was studying over his bleeding knuckles, then brought his eyes up to meet mine, grinning.

"You've been my best teacher so far, Eddie." I patted the empty seat again. "Who do you think inspired me to study biology in school?" He leapt on the porch and took his usual spot beside me on the swing.

"You're a natural-born teacher," I added. Suddenly, my perch began to swing back and forth. Eddie was in a better mood.

"Do you know who Rudy Mancke is?" I asked.

"One of them Wofford boys, I reckon." There was just a little hint of bitterness in his voice.

"Nope." I brushed his mocking tone aside. "He's a biology teacher from Spartanburg. Quite passionate—reminds me a little of you," I took his abused hand from his lap. "I bet he'll be famous someday." Examining both sides of his hand, I wondered out loud. "Why don't you use gloves when you work?"

Eddie shrugged. "How's that—him putting you in mind of me?"

I told Eddie how Rudy came to Converse as a guest lecturer sometimes. On one of these visits we took a night excursion to the lake at Camp Croft. We paddled around in johnboats near the shore to look for some nightlife we missed in the light of day. "You know how the mountain is different at night," I said.

"Yup. It's a whole nuther place." He nodded, showing appreciation, stretched his arms out to grab the chains, and pushed the swing way back with his long legs. "Draw your legs up," he said.

I pulled my feet up and hooked my heels on the front of the swing. Eddie pushed off and bent his legs up under the seat. The swing whooshed forward and groaned. We let the momentum carry us back and forth for a long time.

"Hey. Do you still sleep outside?" I asked when the creaking swing stopped.

"More often than not," he said.

I snorted. "My friends at school can't believe my best friend is a wild mountain boy. Er ... man. I mean mountain man."

"I ain't wild," he said and chuckled.

"Actually, you're the most civilized, disciplined person I know."

"I hope you're not going wild off at college." He wasn't laughing this time.

"Wild? Off at college? Converse is a mile from our house behind the mill. I live at home. Eddie, please don't start that again." I hung my head and shook it. "Besides, I have to do well to keep my scholarship."

"Sorry." Eddie took a couple of deep breaths. "Oh, you were telling me about the trip to the lake," he reminded me, nudged my shoulder with his, and took my hand back.

"Well, I held the spotlight for our boat and pointed it where they told me to. This snake swam across the beam and Rudy saw it. He told T.R. Stokes, my partner, to paddle over and try to grab the snake. T.R. missed it. Then Rudy dove—well, more like belly flopped out of his boat and grabbed the snake. That man is fast."

Eddie was intent on the story, grinning big. "Rudy rose up from the water and lifted the snake up at eye level. Water was dripping from his hair into his eyes and mouth as he showed it off. Then he announced to the class, 'Ladies and gentleman, this is a red-bellied water snake, more common around these parts than people think!' He ran his hand down the length of the snake's body and said, 'Ahh, we have a male.'

"I was hoping nobody would ask, but one girl did, and I made a face and groaned. 'How do you know it's a male, Rudy?'

"Rudy said, 'See this lump right here?' and he pointed at the snake's belly. 'Under this lump are the snake's penises.'"

"'Penises!' about a half dozen girls squealed all together."

Eddie sat beside me on the swing, his chest quivering with suppressed laughter while I finished my tale.

"Then Rudy squeezed the poor thing between his fingers and caused the young gentleman snake to expose his dual genitalia to all those fine young Converse women. They all gasped," I said, laughing. "One girl wailed, 'They're jagged!'

"Rudy just stood there exposing the snake and grinning like he was showing off a prize. So I helped in the lecture and told her it was to keep the lady snake from slithering away before the deed was done. Just like you told me when we were twelve. They thought it was the most disgusting thing, and T.R. said, 'That's gotta hurt.'"

Eddie was choking with laughter and dabbed his eyes with the pinched-up neck of his sweaty t-shirt. He shook his head. "I wouldn't a done that in a crowd of mixed company like *he* did," Eddie said when he finally wound down.

"I know. Like I said, you're more civilized than most people, Eddie. Or maybe modest?"

He shrugged and snorted. And we sat and rocked. ✶

WHEN THE LEASE IS UP

▸ KAM NEELY

Grady pulled up to the cow gate, which had faded a dark brown and rusted off the hinges. The metal tubing had the prickly undulations of sprayed stucco. Someone had knocked over the four-by-six walk-through on the right side of the gate, and he could see ATV tracks still fresh in the red clay. He grabbed his yellow boots out of the back and laced them up, leaving the last two holes undone. A mossy stretch, only a few hundred yards down from the entrance, remained shady year round, and a small spring ran across the road. The road was slick all the way down to the gully because of the spring. At the bottom of the hill lay a corrugated metal culvert, cast out into the woods by a flash flood that had also washed out the wooden bridge. The treated utility poles that had served as the runners were thrown down the gully like two matchsticks, showing that once water starts moving ain't much what can stop it.

His uncle, E.W., had sent Grady down here to the farm mostly because Grady owed the ornery son-of-a-bitch a chunk of money that went missing from his trailer four months back. He knew his nephew had spent it on pills, and now he was intent on the boy working it off. E.W. never could prove anything, but he'd seen Grady living high on the hog with all kinds of girls and booze and because Grady hadn't come around lately, bumming him for cash. The boy never did put up a fight about it, and E.W. took his silence as an admission of guilt.

E.W. had sent Grady down here to meet his man, Mike, who he'd known since his old army days and who, his uncle told him, was interested in buying a hunting lease.

"So, you and Clary are the only two what still have a stake in the farm?" Mike asked E.W. one day a month or so back, after looking at a rough plat of the place.

"Us and our heirs. I tell you what, Mike, they ain't much land like it left around here—one-hundred-and-sixty-seven acres of hardwoods right off Foster Chapel Road. Been passed down three generations."

"What do you reckon you and Clary could get for it?"

"Clary, he don't want to sell. We had it logged three times in three different phases in the last ten years. Last time around it brought close to $12,000. The timber rights alone pay the taxes and what little maintenance there is, plus some."

"And your brother is content to let it ride, just like that?"

"Who, Clary? He ain't got the foggiest about income from the timber. He thinks it's a break even affair after property taxes. All he told me was to make sure the loggers didn't cut this stand of hardwoods down by Otts Shoals Creek." E.W. pointed to a spot on the plat that showed the outline of a free-standing structure. "Something about the deer moving someplace else if we weren't careful."

E.W. walked away for a spell, and Mike continued to look down at the plat.

"But I got some other plans for the farm. Plans you and me need to talk about."

Clary had been in a wheelchair going on close to ten years. His place had become a real dump. He called in his painkillers every two weeks to the VA and sent Grady to pick 'em up. He must have known he was setting his son up, but all he could do was offer a meek warning one day before the boy headed out with the prescription tucked in his back pocket.

"Grady, see what this shit has done to your old man? I can't go anywhere without them damn pills."

Clary didn't go anywhere to speak of anyway. And he wasn't much company, for that matter. He sat in the den most of the day, drinking

Bud Lite, taking his medications, and watching game shows, dreaming he might still have a chance to make it big if someone would just call his number. Every couple of hours he would roll himself out to the rickety back stoop that Grady had built one summer and smoke two cigarettes in a row.

E.W. was running things now, as far as the family was concerned, and what was left of the paving business. Grady knew that his family used to be rich, or so they told him around town. When Pop died, Clary and E.W. each got twelve acres on Fairforest Creek, on top of the land at the farm, but E.W. talked his brother into selling off the majority of it as individual lots while keeping for each of them just enough for a trailer and a nice fenced-in section for the dogs. When things was still going good and Pop was still alive, Clary took Grady down to their two-acre lot and set his son beside him on the bulldozer. He cranked the thing up, and his son could hardly hear him over the diesel engine.

"Here, Grady. We're gonna finally put some roots down. Right here." And this he says while he's mowing over white oaks, sweet gums, poplar, and dogwoods. One set of roots going in, and the other coming out, splintering in protest.

Turns out neither E.W. nor Clary had Pop's business sense. At one time they was running a grading and paving operation with five dump trucks, two excavators, a bulldozer, two caterpillars, and three pavers. Pop had got in tight with one of his World War II buddies on the State Transportation Board and had landed a bevy of sweet highway contracts. Didn't matter really how it turned out, because it was state work. "Good enough for government work" was his official motto. But E.W. and Clary quickly ran the thing into the ground after Pop was gone. Pretty soon the bank came and took all the heavy equipment except for one Bobcat and one F700 dump bed, and E.W. bought his brother out of the business for next to nothing. All Clary and Grady was left with was their lot and trailer, and Lord only knows how he and E.W. had sense enough to hang on to the old farm.

Grady got the cow gate open easy enough, and Mike, the man sent down by E.W., pulled up and parked off on the shoulder of the highway right in front of the speed limit sign. He got out slowly, like he was sore from a long drive, and came over. Grady didn't know Mike well, having seen him only a few times at E.W.'s place, mostly when he had come to hit his uncle up for cash. Mike looked the boy up and down.

"You got your gun?"

"Huh?"

"Your rifle, or shotgun or something?"

"What for?"

"What for? In case they's someone already in there hunting. I can see one stand from here. I can tell you right off they's been people in here on a regular basis. Look here ... look at the size of that boot print. That ain't no kid sneaking off in the woods with a six pack and his new girl. That's the print of someone loaded down with thirty or forty pounds of gear."

Grady went back to the truck and looked in the back and on his gun rack.

"Must've left them in the trailer."

They walked around the rusting gate and headed down the muddy logging road, in the direction of the washed-out bridge.

Grady wadn't entirely truthful when he told people about the pills. He told them his old man got him hooked on that and alcohol both. It started, he said, because everything was so laid back at home—how he could crack one open right in front of his dad and sit down on the couch next to his wheelchair, and the old man didn't seem to give a rip. Grady chalked it up to genetics. He knew his dad was drinking beer with Pop before he finished high school and imagined that Pop had no problem getting loaded in front of his two boys and letting the old war stories fly. At some point, Clary and E.W. had learned to clear out before things got out of hand, displaying a natural instinct for survival.

"People was drawn to your Pop, even if he was a drunk," Clary had told his son a while back. "On account of that, I guess—his like-ability—he made a good name in his business. But he was sloppy, liked to get through the jobs quick and get paid. I'm the first to admit, me and E.W. got the sloppy and none of the savvy. We got the kick-back beer drinking and carrying on and none of the work ethic. Let me tell you something, Grady, your Pop knew how to put in a long day, even if it was beer coming out of his pores instead of sweat."

It was E.W.'s son, Barry, who got Grady onto the painkillers. Barry was shopping pills for him before he even knew what was in his dad's prescription. Barry was Grady's only cousin, and he pulled him down into the lowlife with him. Everyone could tell Grady had liked school from the get go and had some knack for it (maybe inherited from Pop's savvy), but Barry knew the hot chicks and where to get the booze and weed, and Grady gravitated to him like everyone else. Pretty soon, Barry was putting his cousin up to taking a handful from his dad's bottle.

"Your old man won't know the difference. He's zoned out half the time anyway, what with beer and pills in his system all the time and staring straight into the flickering light of his TV. He'll just keep calling it in, and the doctors'll figure he's in more pain, or addicted, like the rest of the amputees who'd served in 'Nam."

"I ain't up for all of that, Barry. I ain't up for doing real time."

"You just pass 'em off. Keep a few for yourself, and I'll take care of the rest. It's easy money, cuz, easy money."

Before too long the two cousins had a racket going, and Grady approached Barry, wondering about their dwindling supplies.

"You talk to your old man and find us two or three other rejects who are signed up to get their pills from the VA. And then you offer to go pick theirs up, too, once every two weeks. They can't argue the point as long as someone calls in first and lets 'em know you're coming. Half of 'em can't drive no how."

Before too long Grady had quit his job and joined up with Barry full time.

Mike was not a big man, but he walked like one. He had a slow gait, like someone headed for trouble, but not scared of it. Just walking slow and steady right up to its face. And his eyes was something else. Bright, piercing blue, like from some other world. Grady was ready to get the whole deal over with, showing the land every other week until somebody took a lease on it, but E.W. continued to hold the missing money over his head. Deep down, E.W. knew his own son, Barry, was running the racket with the pills and that Grady was the innocent bystander who had got sucked into the mess. First thing after the money disappeared, E.W. kicked Barry out.

"He's practically shacked up with his girl anyhow," E.W. had told one of his buddies at the concrete plant. "A skinny chick with stringy hair and knobbed-off fingernails. A real dopehead. I imagine it's working out good for her, too," he said thinking of the fact that she probably had access to more painkillers than she knew what to do with. E.W. knew Barry had used the missing money to buy more pills. The supply lines were drying up, and some of the veterans Grady went to see were starting to question how their bottles had come up empty so soon. But E.W. stayed after Grady. Every couple of days, he was calling for him to run over to the store in Eutawville or feed the dogs when he was off turkey hunting. Grady figured he would eventually work the thing off and then his uncle would quit calling, but he was beginning to wonder who was keeping track of the tally and if it would end sometime soon after all.

Mike and Grady made it up out of the second gulley. Mike kept lumbering on, so Grady went out in front, hoping to speed things up.

"Lots of good tracks. I seen some fox, deer, and three toms."

"Nice deer on the land for sure. You can tell they's heavy bucks around when you see the prongs behind the front hooves. Means they's a lot of weight pushing down into the mud."

"Nice and quiet back here, too. I believe the old cabin should be close by somewhere. Maybe off to the right a quarter mile or so."

"E.W.'s done showed me the property lines. I told him I would do it for five an acre, and he came back with seven. We settled on six. Said none of you hunt the property anymore. Might as well let me on it so we keep the other folks out."

Mike stripped off his safety vest. Grady looked back, and the man stared him down. His sharp blue eyes pierced right through Grady, as if God himself was looking through the boy's soul. Mike had a close-shaved head, and small beads of sweat were beginning to form all around his scalp. He wore a white V-neck undershirt, and it was the cleanest white Grady had ever seen. Like he was sent down to deliver a message straight from heaven, and the Lord up above was the one doing his laundry.

"They did what they said."

"Do what?"

"The loggers. They did what they said. They promised my dad they would leave the hardwoods over there to the right for the deer. You can see one of the old shade trees that was part of the main farmhouse. All that's left is the cabin. Looks right out over Otts Shoals creek. We used to come up here with Pop when we was kids. Me and Barry would sleep out here with him during deer season. We could hear acorns falling on the metal roof of the cabin all night it seems like. We're almost there."

Mike looked behind them for the first time, and Grady could tell he was growing anxious about something, as if he was counting their steps.

"We won't stay long. I just want to see the old cabin. Hell, man, I haven't been up here in ... must be about five years."

Grady was looking for a way through the thicket. He could see the front porch of the cabin and could tell that the woodshed roof had fallen over behind of it. He stepped back onto the logging road to find another way around and backed right into Mike. Grady turned around halfway, but the tattooed man was on him in a flash. He reached in the back of his pants and pulled out a .45 pistol. Grady tried to take off through the briars, but Mike grabbed him in a half nelson around the throat and held the pistol to his head.

"I'm sorry, boy, real sorry. Your uncle had other plans for you."

"My uncle?"

"Your own flesh and blood," he laughed as he said this.

"Can someone tell my dad? Make something up for him at least?"

"Barry is taking care of him as we speak."

"Barry? But I thought E.W. and Barry wadn't ..."

For the first time Mike grinned and loosened his grip on Grady's throat.

"I believe they's trying to clean up the family tree, if you know what I'm driving at. They ain't after no hunting lease, son, they want your land. All of it."

For the first time, Grady realized his lease was up, too. Mike grinned again, and Grady could see the glint of several gold crowns from deep in the man's throat. It must be miles from here to there, Grady thought, entranced by the golden reflection. Mike's grip tightened and the pistol was cool against the boy's temple. Grady thought for a second of the man's t-shirt: that it wouldn't look so clean after what was coming. But then again, he probably could have guessed that Mike had stashed another one close by, and that it was just as white and clean, like an angel's. ✳

HOME TO TARA

➤ BETTY BURGIN SNOW

"Golden Years Retreat, where your golden years are your most colorful years." Assistant Manager Jen Fowler was manning the phone. "How may I help you?"

"How's Mama today?" Ethel Charles didn't have to identify herself. She and Jen had known each other all their lives.

"You mean Miss Scarlett?" Jen asked, chuckling. "Oh, she's fine. I wish we could get her to eat more, though. Why, she's nothing but skin and bones."

Ethel sighed. "I know," she said. "Mama wants a seventeen-inch waistline like Scarlett O'Hara's. I'm surprised she hasn't asked for Mammy to come lace up her corset."

"That'll probably be next." Jen said. "This morning during Creativity Time your mother made a fan out of her art paper. She kept fluttering it in front of her face and battin' her eyelashes at old Mr. Simmons."

Ethel groaned. "She thinks she's a *belle*. Pathetic, isn't it?"

"Oh, I don't know," Jen said. "She's still attractive with that silver hair and those green eyes. 'Course, I remember what a looker she used to be—long legs, hour- glass figure …"

Ethel surveyed her own short, stocky reflection in the glass patio doors. *Dad's genes*, she thought, running her free hand through wiry, putty-colored hair. *Spittin' image.*

Jen's laughter jarred her back to the present. "Mr. Simmons was oblivious to Dolly's charms," she was saying. "Snoring so hard he was fluttering his beard and scattering toast crumbs everywhere."

"Oh, Lord," Ethel said, taking deep breaths. "Did they ever get Mama back on track?"

"Nope," Jen said. "Every time the art teacher tried to get Miss Dolly to draw something, she'd say, 'Fiddle-dee-dee. I'll think about that tomorrow.' You know, it's amazing how she can sound just like Vivien Leigh in the movie. Oh, hang on a minute, Ethel. I've got to take this call."

On hold, Ethel recalled how it had irked her when her mother started aping the British actress's version of Southern speech. "Nobody in upstate South Carolina talks like that," Ethel told her husband, Bert. "It's just an affectation. I'll put a stop to it." Ethel began speaking to Dolly in rough, uneducated English. "Hit ain't time fer yer medicine yit," she might say, or, "Them biscuits is fixin' to burn."

One day Dolly stamped her little foot. "Great balls of fire," she said. "I never thought I'd find one of those trashy Slatterys inside my house." She shook her finger at Ethel. "And call me Miss Scarlett, you hear?"

From then on, Dolly instructed everyone to call her Scarlett. Ethel's dad and most of their friends complied with affectionate good humor; Ethel did not. "I'm not going to encourage her," she said. "Mama's got to come to her senses."

"Was there something you needed, Hon?" Jen was back on the line. "There's another call waiting."

"Tomorrow's Mama's eighty-third birthday," Ethel said. "I'd like to come over with a cake. Enough for everyone."

Papers rustled on the other end. "That'll be fine," Jen said. "You can use the dining room, but don't come at mealtime. How about two o'clock?"

Ethel jotted the time on her calendar. "Thanks, Jen," she said. "See you tomorrow."

Dolly's descent into dementia had begun during what Ethel called her mother's "literary phase." In her prime, Dolly was something of a local celebrity, famous for her annual "book parties." Guests were invited to portray a character from a well-known novel. Dolly always acted the juiciest parts herself. She'd played Becky Thatcher, Becky Sharp, Emma Bovary, Anna Karenina, even Lady Chatterley, but Scarlett O'Hara from *Gone with the Wind* captured her imagination like none of the others.

Events in the novels dictated the venue of the parties. Dolly reserved a ballroom, a hunting lodge, an ante-bellum mansion, or—in the case of *Tom Sawyer*—an entire park. Invitations were coveted, but then Dolly repeated her *Gone with the Wind* party two years in a row, and the year after that.

Gradually, fewer people accepted Dolly's hand-written invitations, which had slipped noticeably in their quality—shaky lettering, vague details of time and place, repetition of role assignments. "I'm not playing Belle Watling again," one frequent guest complained. "Why can't someone else play the prostitute for a change?"

Ethel's dad covered for his wife as best he could. "You know how Dolly loves that book," he'd say. "And it's so long! Dolly says we haven't even scratched the surface." But Dad's loyalty couldn't conceal what was happening to Dolly. "Remember Don Quixote?" he asked Ethel. "He read so many books of chivalry that, as Cervantes put it, he 'fried his brain.' The old fella thought he was a knight-errant." He smiled. "He caused all kinds of mayhem riding around on an old nag looking for wrongs to right."

Ethel could see the similarities. Her mother had caused some mayhem of her own at what turned out to be the final book party. Ethel was always on hand to help out at these events, but Bert would have no part of it. "I have enough problems," he often said. "Why would I pretend to have somebody else's?" And he'd shake his head at such folly. Ethel drew the line at playing a role too, but she made herself useful behind the scenes, seeing that food and drink preparations flowed smoothly. In recent years her primary task was helping her dad keep an eye on Dolly.

The Mayor had accepted an invitation, quite a social *coup* for Dolly. "His Honor has agreed to play Ashley Wilkes," she told her husband. "Won't everybody be pea-green with envy?"

Dolly descended the staircase of the rented, restored Southern mansion the night of the party, dressed in a green velvet ball gown. "Just something Mammy made from the drapes," she said, in answer to admiring remarks. She and the Rhett Butler of the evening enacted the scene at the jail when Scarlett asks Rhett for money to pay the taxes on Tara.

During the applause, Ethel slipped into the dining room, where caterers were adding final touches to banquet tables. The meal would follow the next scene, Scarlett's farewell to Ashley before his return to the battlefield.

A commotion erupted from the ballroom. Gasps, squeals, scuffling, a thud, like someone falling. Ethel threw open the double doors to see her mother prostrate, arms clasped around the Mayor's knees. Ethel's dad was struggling to loosen Dolly's grip. With every step he took, the Mayor dragged Dolly along, her voluminous skirts sweeping the floor like a velvet broom. Dolly was wailing, "Oh, Ashley, don't go. Ashley, oh, Ashley."

Finally free, the disheveled Mayor looked down on Dolly, sobbing at his feet. His wife, who'd came as plain, spinsterish India Wilkes, snatched up her wraps and hustled her husband out with the skimpiest of goodbyes. Ethel's dad followed them. "I'm so sorry," he said, hands pleading. "My wife gets a little carried away sometimes."

Ethel helped Dolly to her feet. "Get up, Mama," she said. "You have guests."

Dolly put a hand to her forehead. "I declare," she said. "I'm afraid I'm feeling faint." Looking straight at Ethel, she added, "Mammy, get me the smelling salts."

The remaining guests, whispering among themselves, made a hasty departure.

Ethel became full-time caregiver the day her dad died of a heart attack. He collapsed while climbing the stairs with Dolly's breakfast tray, complete with red rose. Ethel tried to take charge. She cleaned Dolly's house, paid her bills, cooked nourishing meals. It wore her down, and she knew she was neglecting Bert. Dolly wasn't going to get any better. Ethel had taken her to a psychiatrist, who attempted to test Dolly's competency level, but she responded to his questions with flirtatious banter. "Well, I declare, if you aren't the handsomest thing," she said. "Now, you be careful fightin' those Yankees, you hear? I'll be waitin' for you."

The doctor, lips twitching, handed Ethel samples of a drug designed to slow dementia. "Your mother shouldn't be living alone," he said. "Maybe you could hire somebody to move in with her."

That evening Ethel presented Bert with an alternate plan. "Let's move Mama here," she said. "It would be lots easier on me, and you and I would have more time together."

Bert agreed, but Ethel sensed he wasn't happy with the arrangement. He had to forego walking around the house in his underwear and could no longer shower and shave in the guest bathroom. Besides, contrary to her prediction, Ethel had even less time for him. "I wish I'd never quit the post office," Bert said. "This is not my idea of retirement."

Dolly wandered around the house day and night, peering out windows, flinching at every noise. "I promised Ashley I'd take care of Mellie," she said. "We're leaving for Tara as soon as her baby's born." She frowned. "And where is Prissy? She knows all about birthin' babies. She told me so."

Ethel no longer attempted to argue her mother out of her delusions. "You need to rest up for the journey," she said. "Lie down for a while, Mama."

"Scarlett," Dolly said.

Bert learned to cope with Dolly's presence by puttering in his workshop or playing cards with his buddies at the firehouse. "There's no fool like an old fool," he'd say after one of Dolly's flights of fantasy.

"That man is a saint," Ethel told her friends. "A lot of husbands would've left home over what Bert's put up with since Mama moved in."

But even Bert had his limit. At supper one evening Dolly refused Ethel's specialty—roast beef with mashed potatoes and gravy. Giggling, she said, "I couldn't eat another bite. Those Tarleton twins just wouldn't take 'no' for an answer when they invited me to a barbecue this afternoon."

"That does it!" Bert's fist hit the table. "I know she's your mama, Ethel, but this is killing you, and it sure as Hell isn't doing me any good."

Ethel protested, but feebly. She knew Bert was right. She was exhausted, and Bert didn't know the half of it. Dolly had begun to wander. Last week, she'd donned a red velour robe belted tightly through the middle, a brunette wig saved from one of the long-ago parties, and red satin high-heeled mules she'd found tossed to the back of Ethel's closet.

Ethel, thinking her mother was napping, picked that moment to take a shower. Bert was at the firehouse. Dolly let herself out the front way, walked up on Mr. Robbins's porch three doors down, and knocked. Mr. Robbins, seeing who it was and knowing something of the circumstances, gallantly offered Dolly his arm and guided her home.

Ethel, who was frantically searching the house and yard, saw them coming: Dolly leaning into Mr. Robbins and gazing up at his homely face; Mr. Robbins, nodding his hairless head and patting her hand.

"Mama," Ethel cried. "Where have you been? I've been looking all over for you." She turned to Mr. Robbins. "I needed some time to take a shower," she said, hands wringing, voice breaking. "I'd just checked on her. She was asleep." She sat down on the porch stoop. "I was about to call the police."

"Calm down, Ethel," Mr. Robbins said. "She's fine. She thought I was Rhett Butler. Said she guessed I'd be carrying her upstairs and having my way with her."

Ethel lowered her face into her hands. "I'm so sorry," she said. "How'd you ever persuade her to leave?"

"Told her there were Yankees in the attic," he said. He flexed an invisible muscle. "Besides, at my age, I didn't think I could carry her upstairs." With a wave, he turned to go.

Dolly called out, "Now, don't you be a stranger, Cap'n Butler. You hear?" Ethel steered her mother toward the house, hoping to get her settled for the night.

At that point Ethel admitted that taking care of Dolly was too much for her. With more than a little nudging from Bert, she made an appointment to tour Golden Years Retreat. Jen showed her around the facility one afternoon while Bert stayed home with Dolly. Ethel liked what she saw and completed an application on the spot. Thanks to Jen, the waiting period was short.

On moving day Dolly's tiny frame fit easily between Ethel and Bert in the cab of the Chevy pickup. Her luggage, which was considerable, lay stacked in the back with a tarp over it. Bert reached over Dolly's lap and squeezed Ethel's hand. "She'll be fine," he said. Ethel nodded, blinking away tears.

When they reached the end of the long oak-shaded driveway leading up to Golden Years, Dolly clasped her hands together. "Home," she said. "I've come home to Tara at last."

Ethel eyed the two-story, white-columned building and shook her head. "I must be getting delusional," she told Bert. "For a minute there I thought I heard the theme song from the movie." Bert grinned.

Entering the lobby, Ethel watched her mother take stock of the crystal chandelier, high ceilings, and heavy draperies. "See there," Dolly said. "I told you the Yankees wouldn't burn Tara."

An attendant stepped forward. "I'm Grace," she said, leading them down a hallway toward Dolly's room. "We've been waiting for you, Miss Dolly."

"Miss Scarlett," Dolly said.

"Of course, Miss Scarlett," Grace said. "Now you just make yourself comfortable. We'll go to the dining room for supper soon."

"Supper?" Dolly said. "But how will I ever decide which young man to eat barbecue with? And what shall I wear?"

Ethel and Bert hung Dolly's clothes and set a few family pictures around. Grace encouraged them to leave. Dolly seemed oblivious when Ethel hugged and kissed her goodbye. "She already feels at home here," Grace said, pressing a tissue into Ethel's hand. They left Dolly searching through the clothes closet.

Ethel and Bert visited every Sunday. Dolly didn't remember them after a while. Once she grabbed Ethel's wrists and examined her hands. "You've been picking cotton without your gloves," she said. "A lady's hands shouldn't feel like a burlap bag."

Now on Dolly's birthday Ethel sat beside Bert in the truck. She held a cake decorated with roses and the words HAPPY BIRTHDAY. "No name," she said to Bert. "She doesn't recognize her own name, and I'll be damned if I'll have them put *Scarlett* on it." She balanced two half-gallon cartons of lemonade between her feet.

"What the Hell," Bert shouted as they pulled into Golden Years' driveway. Ethel lurched against her seat belt as the truck screeched to a stop. Lemonade cartons toppled onto her feet. The cake box bounced against the dashboard then back onto her knees.

"Oh my God!" Ethel yelled, handing Bert the cake, jumping from the truck, and bolting toward the building. The parking lot of Golden Years was crowded with fire trucks. Police cars sprawled on the grass, while the back doors of an ambulance gaped open to dislodge a stretcher. A barricade of sawhorses surrounded the whole area.

"My mother lives here," Ethel shouted to a paramedic. Shoving him aside, she pushed through a jumble of fire hoses, yellow-slickered firemen, and white-coated medical personnel. She saw residents on the grass, some in wheelchairs or on stretchers, others standing, bewildered expressions on their faces.

Ethel snatched the arm of a sturdy-looking nurse. "What happened?" she asked, gulping for breath. Bert arrived, huffing and puffing, still holding the cake.

"It's not as bad as it looks," the nurse said, covering an old man's thin shoulders with a blanket. "A small fire in the kitchen." She raised a cup of water to the man's trembling mouth. "Just take small sips," she said, wiping his lips. "By the way," she said, turning back to Ethel. "If it hadn't been for your mama, things might have been much worse."

Ethel stared at her. "What do you mean?"

"Well, it was lunchtime, so everybody was in the dining room. Miss Dolly was agitated about something, couldn't be still, and wouldn't eat a bite. She kept leaving her chair, muttering something about the Yankees." The nurse shrugged. "Of course, that's all she ever talks about, so nobody paid any attention."

Ethel nodded. "What did she do?" she asked.

"Well, you know, she's spry for her age," the nurse said. "Before anyone could stop her, she climbed on top of her chair and screamed at the top of lungs, 'Don't you smell the smoke? The Yankees are coming. They're burning Atlanta.'"

Ethel swayed against Bert. "Well, that got our attention," the nurse continued. "And, sure enough, a grease fire was burning on the stove. The staff put it out with a fire extinguisher, but we had to call the fire department and evacuate the building. State rules."

"Can we go inside?" Bert asked.

The nurse shook her head. "Not until the firemen give the signal. Your mama's over there." She pointed to some ambulatory residents gathered around a policeman writing on a clipboard.

Ethel walked toward the group. She heard Dolly's voice. "Why Cap'n Butler," she was saying, tapping the officer on his chest with her paper pleated fan. "How you do run on. Of course, I'll dance with you—but only for the Cause."

Ethel put her arm around her mother's shoulders. "Happy Birthday, Scarlett," she whispered. ✳

ABOUT THE AUTHORS

KATHRYN A. BRACKETT, a native of Spartanburg, holds a BA degree in English with a concentration in creative writing from Converse College and an MFA in fiction from the University of Pittsburgh. She has published in *Borderlands Magazine* and received an honorable mention in the 2003 Stony Brook Short Fiction Prize. She recently finished a short story collection, *Places Like This*, and is working on a novel.

CHRISTOPHER BUNDY's stories and essays have appeared or are forthcoming in *Atlanta Magazine, Glimmer Train Stories, Ellery Queen Mystery Magazine, The Rambler, Creative Loafing, The Dos Passos Review*, and others. Chris, who grew up in Spartanburg, is a founding editor of the literary journal *New South* and lives in Atlanta.

ELIZABETH COX has published four novels: *Familiar Ground, The Ragged Way People Fall Out Of Love, Night Talk*, and *The Slow Moon*. She also has published a collection of short stories, *Bargains in the Real World*, and one of these stories was chosen for the 1994 O. Henry Collection. She has also published poems and essays in *The Oxford American, Southern Review*, and elsewhere. She shares the John Cobb Chair of Humanities with her husband, C. Michael Curtis, at Wofford College in Spartanburg.

LOU DISCHLER, formerly a painter, sculptor, and inventor, is presently at work on his seventh novel. He lives in Spartanburg.

SAM HOWIE's fiction and nonfiction have appeared in such publications as *Shenandoah, The Writer's Chronicle, Fiction International, Potomac Review,* and *Southern Humanities Review.* His collection of stories, *Rapture Practice,* was published by Main Street Rag in fall 2009. He is an instructor and director of the Writing Center at Converse College.

A descendant of the settlers to the Carolina backwoods, CAROL ISLER has received her BA in history from Converse College and an M. Ed from Lesley University. She teaches chemistry at James F. Byrnes High School. A resident of Lyman, South Carolina, she is a winner of the Hub City Prize in poetry, and her work has been published in *Catfish Stew* and *The Petigru Review.*

JEREMY L. C. JONES is a freelance writer, editor, and part-time professor living in his wife's hometown of Spartanburg. He is on the board of the South Carolina Academy of Authors, HubCulture Inc., and is the interview editor for the Southern Nature Project. He is the founding director of Shared Worlds at Wofford College, a creative writing and world-building summer program for high school students.

WENDY KING was born in Anderson, South Carolina, and currently resides in Spartanburg. She received an MFA from Arizona State University in 2000 and has previously published in *So To Speak,* a feminist journal of language and arts.

MARILYN KNIGHT teaches creative writing at the University of South Carolina Upstate. She is the author of a novel, *Babydoll* (1988), and assorted shorter works. She lives in Spartanburg with her husband, Donald, three dogs, and twelve cats, all rescue animals.

MOLLY KNIGHT grew up in downtown Spartanburg and spent her formative years at the Spartanburg Day School. She currently lives in Durham, North Carolina, where she is working on her PhD in German Studies at Duke University.

JOHN LANE teaches English and environmental studies at Wofford College. "Before the Chicken's Fried" was a winner in the inaugural South Carolina Fiction Project in 1984. Since that first contest two more stories have won as well. He has three books of prose from the University of Georgia Press, and his latest book is *The Best of the Kudzu Telegraph*, published by the Hub City Writers Project.

THOMAS MCCONNELL's work has appeared in *Connecticut Review*, *Cortland Review*, *Calabash*, and *Yemassee*, among other publications, and he has won prizes in the Porter Fleming Awards competition for Fiction, Essay, and Drama, and the South Carolina Fiction Project. He is also the winner of the Hub City Prize for Fiction and the H.E. Francis Award. His collection of stories, *A Picture Book of Hell and other Landscapes*, was published by Texas Tech University Press in 2005. He teaches at the University of South Carolina Upstate.

KAM NEELY, a Spartanburg native, has studied at Furman University, University College Dublin, the Johann-Wolfgang Goethe University and the University of North Carolina at Chapel Hill. He has published fiction and poetry in several university journals. He currently works in a business founded by his great-grandfather in 1923 and lives with his wife, Emily, and two sons on Spartanburg's Eastside. "The Lease is Up" won the 2009 Hub City Prize for Fiction.

THOMAS PIERCE grew up in Spartanburg and graduated from Wofford College. While there, he received the Benjamin Wofford Prize for Fiction, which resulted in the publication of his novella, *said the dark fishes* (Holocene Press, 2005.) He currently lives in Washington, D.C., and works as a producer and freelance reporter for National Public Radio.

A native of Massachusetts, NORMAN POWERS lived and worked in Manhattan for twenty-five years at the National Video Center as a film and television writer and producer for his own New York-based production company, Chelsea Lane Productions. Residing in Landrum,

South Carolina, since 1992, Norm devotes much of his free time to free-lance writing and is a past winner of the Hub City Prize for Creative Nonfiction.

ROSA SHAND's novel, *The Gravity of Sunlight*, was named a *New York Times* Notable Book of the Year and won both the Best Fiction and Best First Fiction Awards from the Texas Institute of Letters. She has published stories in *Virginia Quarterly Review*, *The Southern Review*, *Shenandoah*, and elsewhere. Now living in Davidson, North Carolina, she is the Larrabee Professor Emerita of English at Converse College and has been Visiting Writer at Wofford College.

After living and teaching in western Pennsylvania for thirty-one years, BETTY BURGIN SNOW returned to Spartanburg to be near her family. She taught English and Spanish at Spartanburg High in the sixties and seventies. When her husband, Rich, took a job at Clarion College in 1973, the couple moved to Oil City, Pennsylvania. She began writing after her retirement from high school teaching in 1997. In "Home to Tara," the main character is loosely based on her mother-in-law's image of herself as the eternal homecoming queen.

MICHEL S. STONE has published about a dozen short stories and is a winner of the Hub City Writers Prize for Fiction as well as *South Carolina Magazine's* Very Short Fiction Contest. Her work has appeared numerous times in the *Raleigh News and Observer's* emerging Southern writer series. She is an alumna of the Sewanee Writers Conference and lives in Spartanburg. Stone recently completed her first novel, *The Crossing*.

SUSAN TEKULVE's short fiction collection, *My Mother's War Stories*, was published by Winnow Press. Her nonfiction and stories have appeared in such journals and publications as *Shenandoah*, *Best New Writing 2007*, *The Indiana Review*, *Puerto del Sol*, *Prairie Schooner*, and others. An associate professor of English at Converse College, she is finishing a novel called *Wilderness Road*.

DENO TRAKAS is the Hoy Professor of American Literature and chair of the English Department at Wofford College. He writes poetry and fiction, and Hub City will publish his nonfiction book on Greeks in Upstate South Carolina, *Because Memory Isn't Eternal*, in 2010. Trakas, whose stories have won multiple times in the South Carolina Fiction Project, grew up in St. Petersburg, Florida.

ACKNOWLEDGMENTS

"In Which Sadie Runs off to India to Find out What the Big Deal Is," by Christopher Bundy was previously published in *Creative Loafing* (Atlanta), January 2002.

"Old Court" by Elizabeth Cox was first read on National Public Radio, then published in *American Short Fiction* (University of Texas Press) and then published in her collection of short stories, *Bargains in the Real World* (Random House).

"Ice" by Sam Howie first appeared in *Potomac Review*, Fall/Winter 2005/2006, published at Montgomery College. It also appears in Howie's 2009 short story collection, *Rapture Practice* (Main Street Rag Publishing).

"You've Changed" by Carol Isler was published under another title, "A Vague Recollection of a Conversation," in *Catfish Stew, Tender Morsels of Fine Southern Literature*, Volume III, the 2005 Anthology of the South Carolina Writers Workshop.

"Before the Chicken's Fried" by John Lane was a winner in the South Carolina Fiction Project and was published in 1984 in the *The State*.

"A Proof for Roxanna" by Thomas McConnell was a winner in the South Carolina Fiction Project and appeared in the *Charleston Post & Courier* on September 24, 2006.

"The Nipper" by Susan Tekulve was originally published in *Best New Writing 2007* (Hopewell Press) and received the journal's Editor's Choice Award.

"Pretty Pitiful God" by Deno Trakas was originally published in *Cimarron Review*, 147 (Spring 2004).

The Hub City Writers Project is a non-profit organization whose mission is to foster a sense of community through the literary arts. We do this by publishing books from and about our community; encouraging, mentoring, and advancing the careers of local writers; and seeking to make Spartanburg a center for the literary arts.

Our metaphor of organization purposefully looks backward to the nineteenth century when Spartanburg was known as the "hub city," a place where railroads converged and departed. At the beginning of the twenty-first century, Spartanburg has become a literary hub of South Carolina with an active and nationally celebrated core group of poets, fiction writers, and essayists. We celebrate these writers—and the ones not yet discovered—as one of our community's greatest assets. William R. Ferris, former director of the Center for Southern Studies, says of the emerging South, "Our culture is our greatest resource. We can shape an economic base...And it won't be an investment that will disappear."

(continued)

Noticing Eden • Majory Heath Wentworth

Noble Trees of the South Carolina Upstate • Mark Dennis, Michael Dirr, John Lane, Mark Olencki

Literary South Carolina • Edwin Epps

Magical Places • Marion Peter Holt

When the Soldiers Came to Town • Susan Turpin, Carolyn Creal, Ron Crawley, James Crocker

Twenty: South Carolina Poetry Fellows • Kwame Dawes, editor

The Return of Radio Free Bubba • Meg Barnhouse, Pate Jobe, Kim Taylor

Hidden Voices • Kristofer Neely, editor

Wofford: Shining with Untarnished Honor, 1854-2004 • Doyle Boggs, JoAnn Mitchell Brasington, Phillip Stone

South of Main • Beatrice Hill, Brenda Lee, compilers

Cottonwood Trail • Thomas Webster, G.R. Davis, Jr., Peter L. Schmunk

Comfort & Joy: Nine Stories for Christmas • Kirk Neely, June Neely Kern

Courageous Kate: A Daughter of the American Revolution • Sheila Ingle

Common Ties • Katherine Davis Cann

Spartanburg Revisited • Carroll Foster, Mark Olencki, Emily L. Smith

This Threshold: Writing on the End of Life • Scott Neely, editor

Still Home: The Essential Poetry of Spartanburg • Rachel Harkai, editor

The Best of Kudzu Telegraph • John Lane

Stars Fell on Spartanburg • Jeremy L.C. Jones & Betsy Wakefield Teter, editors

Ask Mr. Smartypants • Lane Filler

Two South Carolina Plays • Jon Tuttle

Through the Pale Door • Brian Ray

A Good Mule Is Hard to Find • Kirk H. Neely

For Here or To Go? • Brandy Lindsey & Baker Maultsby, photography by Carroll Foster & Jeffrey Young